In Love!
With Him

Jagruti Gandhi

Ukiyoto Publishing

All global publishing rights are held by

Ukiyoto Publishing

Published in 2023

Content Copyright © Jagruti Gandhi

ISBN 9789360169374

*All rights reserved.
No part of this publication may be reproduced, transmitted, or stored in a retrieval system, in any form by any means, electronic, mechanical, photocopying, recording or otherwise, without the prior permission of the publisher.*

The moral rights of the authors have been asserted.

This is a work of fiction. Names, characters, businesses, places, events, locales, and incidents are either the products of the author's imagination or used in a fictitious manner. Any resemblance to actual persons, living or dead, or actual events is purely coincidental.

This book is sold subject to the condition that it shall not by way of trade or otherwise, be lent, resold, hired out or otherwise circulated, without the publisher's prior consent, in any form of binding or cover other than that in which it is published.

www.ukiyoto.com

Dedication

Dedicated to all my experiences, failures; up and downs in life. They teach you a lot and more about your surroundings.

To my Mom and Dad; love you for always being there by my side. To my friends and family: You all may be frenzied but even if I got to choose. I'd still choose to be with you.

Thanks to everyone on the Ukiyoto publishing team who helped me so much. Special thanks to my ever-patient publishing team members and also my innovative cover designer.

Having an idea and turning it into a book is as hard as it sounds. The experience is both internally challenging and rewarding. I especially want to thank every individual that helped to make this happen...
I want to thank EVERYONE who ever said anything positive or negative to me or taught me something, I heard it all and it meant something.

And finally, as I have amateur writing skills; I appreciated the valuable reading time of my bibliomaniacs.

Contents

"There He Was…."	1
Escape	4
Meeting Him!	20
On- Offs…	41
Baby Steps…	107
And The Final Fall For Him…	131
About the Author	*143*

"There He Was…."

"I didn't want to fall in love, not at all. But at some point, you smiled and holy shit, I blew it… "

He was walking down the aisle. Kevin; the most handsome and precious man was wearing the most elegant solid blue skinny-fit blazer. The jacket, underpinnings, cufflinks, and the white boutonniere on his suit with his brown eyes glinting in the sunlight like a 'Greek God'. He spiked warm short black hair, and his soft sharp lips were very attractive and captivating. I wanted to touch it; when he comes close but decided not to do so and let out a sigh; adjusting the pace of my heartbeat. The song from my favorite soundtrack 'Glasgow Love theme' from 'Love Actually' added personal touch to the ceremony.

Families and friends united; were seen doing full justice to the smoked crawfish sandwiches and meat patties. The lawn we chose was beside an open restaurant facing the lake view with a breathtaking sunset. Everyone there celebrated LOVE and joy. And I'm in an old-fashioned black suit waiting for him to be near me as soon as possible. "Is it okay"; I asked. "You look incredible" said Kevin kissing my forehead. Kevin's mom came along. We both then walked down to the podium to take vows.

"Good evening and welcome, we are here to celebrate the Kevin and Rohan union. Honor their love, and commitment to each other. And the reading of the ceremony started with Rhea, my best man ever. "He is not perfect; you aren't either and the two will never be perfect but if it can make you giggle at least once; hold onto him; give him the most you can. Don't hurt, don't change, and don't expect more than he can give. Smile when he makes you happy; yell when he makes you mad. Miss him when he is not there. Love when there is loved to be had…

Because perfect guys don't exist, but there is always one guy who is perfect for you. And with that speech, she made even Kevin's eyes numb.

There, all back flashes, how I met him, how did we come together and now everything has fallen in place…

While making vows; all moments had come to stand- still. This is happening, to whom I gave my heart; the most lovable man is with me and will be there for life.

Just in time to kiss, I move forward and Kevin slapped me so hard which brought me back to reality. Everything just vanished except Kevin standing in front of our café. When I had fallen head over heels in love with him; there he was hanging with my love story…

"A perfect couple e is just two imperfect people who refuse to give up on each other."

Escape

"Sometimes I just wanna fly away from here…"

"May I have your attention; please! We shall be landing in New York in another fifteen minutes. Fasten the seat belts and don't smoke. Thank you"; the air hostess announcement brought me back from thoughts before leaving my country.

After some time, we landed. I took a cab straight to the flat assigned by my work center. It was 4ish in the afternoon till I reached 6th Avenue Street. All the buildings are so high that the whole of NYC can be seen in one go…!!

The 21st-floor flat of my building was high- a tech studio apartment. The mesmerizing view peeping through the window got me into my thoughts again; "Why do parents refuse to see what the child desiring for??"

"Why do they stop being a father once we grow up?"

As a kid, they fulfill all our wishes; if you need a 'toy car'; they will happily buy it for us and say,

"There you go kiddo!! Be happy!!"

But as we grow, the restrictions grow bigger. "You can do this, you can't do that", "Don't argue!" Why there are conflicts in our thoughts as we grow up. They start playing as Hitler, influencing… Ah! No!! No!! Rather controlling our thoughts, feelings, and emotion without a compassionate antidote; leave everything dead and empty inside the heart that it throws you into self-hate and self-rejection.

"I don't want to get married", that is what I said to my father which gave a start-off to family melodrama.

"That's the perfect next thing to do in your life once you hatch a higher prospectus job", was the rebuke made by my father.

The doorbell rang and brought me again to reality. It was my luggage. Took the bags in, and knew that will get less time on the weekend as there are meetings and welcome parties that must be attended. So, unpacked all the stuff and started placing the things in the cupboard. Arranged some work-related documents near the side table, and made some arrangements for the first day of the workplace. I didn't know how time passed; it was dinner time. I thought of walking down, a nearby area and then take away. When the evaluator reached downstairs, there was a sweet old lady in mid 50' s. She was cute with a small bob-cut and little curly hair wearing a beautiful simple dress with a floral print on it. She had some bags in her hand. I guess she had done groceries for a couple of weeks. Being human, I offered her help. She gave me a look of astonishment and then followed with a big smile. We came up again to her floor. We took all the bags inside her apartment.

"Mrs. Roy", she said handing the glass of water to me. She thanked me for help as she has been for a couple of years in the building. Staying for so long, still she was only familiar with a few in the neighborhood. She realizes that only she talking for while now. She smiled and asked for my name. I introduced myself to her and as she was the first person in an unknown land, we exchanged numbers so that I could stay in touch with someone in the neighborhood. I requested to recommend some eating outlets. She provided a few names but insisted on staying in as she above to make dinner. It would be a nice change for her as well. She said that she stays alone as her husband died a while ago due to a long medical illness; also, her only son in some tragedy. He was in a law enforcement agency. I was touched that she must have gone through a lot but still has a lovely smile on her face and her willingness to do better for society. I offered her a helping hand to make dinner; she kindly refuses the same. But if you can join me for dinner at times; then she will let me help next time. While we were having a conversation over dinner, I got know that she works for some local NGO. She is also a counselor for high school. I told her my side story as to how I got the job and little notability for my work to fetch a job in a highly renowned firm 'Silverman Financial, Inc', as 'Senior Financial Analyst', also a newbie to the city. I will join the firm tomorrow.

She guided me about a few places I could explore and try different cuisines to dig in…

I thanked her for a lovely dinner. Before leaving, she brought a candy jar and told me took pick one. I picked one; got myself a chocolate candy with a heart-shaped! In an instant, she said 'love' will find you soon…!!

Don't let it go. I didn't get any of it. Mrs. Roy explained that she does this while counseling the kids and sometimes they just need a simple push that motivates them to work hard for what they desire...!! The jar had a lot of shapes like kites, flowers, lions, coins, birds, and more. She believed each shape would depict some near upcoming moments in the person's life. I was curious about what other shapes depicted but decided to keep it for later. I smiled, thanked her for the dinner, and wished each other good night. I headed to my flat with a little more than a content heart. Opening the door put keys on the side table; looked at candy and tossed it on the table remembering Mrs. Roy saying, "Love will find soon…" I too smiled at myself.

Now, I was really tired and jumped on my bed after changing clothes. Thanked Mrs. Roy, for not letting me stay hungry. My eyes were heavy so quickly dozed off.

My eyes didn't bother to open up, but the morning alarm started buzzing which made me alert for my first day. I got dressed up after taking the bath. Made myself a coffee and sandwich which is good for a start who only does basic kitchen cooking; made an extra one and packed it for Mrs. Roy as well. She helped a lot yesterday. I quickly checked the house and switched off AC. Locked the door and went downstairs. She was getting ready for school. I wished her 'Good Morning' and gave her the sandwich. She thanked me for the lovely gesture. I had to take her leave as she had a little more time to abscond for work. I wanted to try the subway but the firm had already made arrangements for the transport for the first day.

Reaching the gate of the workplace, I felt like dreamland is on my way. The gate was beautiful and the building view was mesmerizing. Of course, it was a big name and has been a brand in the industry for more than 15 years. Got to reception, and took my visit card for today; I was straight taken to the HR dept to the HR manager 'Ms. Rhea Lawama' who had been in touch with the first round of interviews itself. We had known each other for more than a month now and we are genuinely happy to see each other. All thanks to our mutual friend Kirin through which we got connected. Now we are friends as well as colleagues. Of course, we had a video interview. But meeting in real was a nice experience. We also gel up very well. Her mom is Indian and settled down in States way long after marrying Rhea's dad. We had 2-3 calls before I reached here but it feels like I have known for a long…!!

Like an old college friend reunion. She is a warm person and welcomed me. She explained to me the rules and regulations of the firm. We did sign a few official documents. Some important other paperwork was also done. After a small conversation about dos and don'ts and remote work policies, she took me to meet other seniors of the departments and fellow workers. First, we met Mr. Robin who had a similar profile to me but a little more experience than me. Got familiar with two of my juniors as well; who will help me throughout all upcoming projects. Finally, I reached my cubicle. Opened the door, it has beautiful overlooking glass nearby my table. The company had a bouquet and a lovely chocolate box arranged on the table. The company surely knows to entertain the newbies. It helps to build a system that motivates an individual's success. Mr. Robin called me to have our first meeting with the client. A client is an old man who is very aggressive about his new venture. We will do a presentation for him so he can take a call on his finances. So, I insist you assist me in 1-2 projects and later you can take over other projects on your own. We were in the meeting room, discussing some pointers for budgeting and other specifications. I felt that every small opportunity was leading to a big one! I will put all my efforts into all given assignments. The client was satisfied with some queries which were to be solved. Robin gave assurance for the same.

After lunch, with some reports writing the day was done. I walked out of my cabin; Rhea joined me from behind. We had a small talk while walking towards the gate about the day spent; she insisted that as its first day, she drop me home. While driving we were listening to 'Backstreet Boys Music.' It was a nice ride. She parked the car near my building. I thanked her for driving me and taking the effort to make me comfortable from day one. She said, "You can get your driving license. It will be useful" I asked to at least get a cup of coffee with me. She refused it, as it was a late but will catch up soon and visit my home. I stepped inside the new home after the first day at work. The silence was new for me but it was overwhelming peace of mind. I entered the bedroom, threw my bag on the desk in the corner to the spacious window, and got dressed in night shorts and a T-shirt; picked up my dry clothes kept in the cupboard. I turned on the idiot box while jumping on the sofa with dinner which was takeaway by me on the way home. I did surf some channels but nothing fun, so started my laptop, chilled on Netflix, gone through some old reports to get prepared for my tomorrow's meeting. I was considerately content with how things have started normalizing here with me. I already neighbor, Rhea who is a colleague cum friend. Good start to new life! My thoughts were interrupted by a cell phone buzz. It was mom. It slipped out mind that it has been whole 2 days since I called her, because of overlook schedule. I already informed her about where I will stay, and how everything is smooth here. Picked up the call, and being a mom, she started firing off questions. She said about how she is missing me, with other enquires from what I ate to how the neighbors were; of course, with some caution like avoiding nightlife with its cons. She came to the same old topic then that I'm sending some photos of a girl; asking her to choose. I didn't want to start with a debate. She got me in her emotional blackmail making me agree to at least go through them. I told her about Rhea and Mrs. Roy, and how they were helpful. I insisted that we can do a video sometime together. I ended the call as I was already sleepy. I didn't know when my eyes got shut which opened the next morning when the doorbell rang.

"Rhea!! Is everything OK??" I exclaimed. She cheerfully entered the house and said that she wanted to have breakfast together for the first day, and wanted to wish you good luck with the very first meeting with my client. I have still given her looks as if this was an invasion of my privacy. She claimed that as you know me for a while, get used to it. I know now that she is a carefree bird, an unexpected shower of rain. But I am happy that we gel up together; siblings that can be partners in everything now!

I prepared a simple breakfast with baked eggs, some orange juice, and oats. Rhea was enjoying the view while digging into the breakfast. I was doing the bed, cleaning the kitchen counter, and making the house tidy and freshened up. I didn't have time for breakfast, so drank a little juice. We left the house while I had an energy bar in one hand and a key in the other. While we were in the car, she was giving small instructions about meeting even if there will assistance. Also, she gave me a firm warning to stay out of sight of Mr. Eric Carter, the chief investment officer. He is very particular about everything. You can crack 3-4 projects before you gain that notability to meet him. You have 'brownie points', once you have delighted him with your work which is a really big task. She wished the best for us, and me hoping the same. We were soon at the gate.

As soon as, we reached our respective workplace; I got a little comfy on my chair and was looking at the desk with a laptop which I was above to open. I got to know from the assistant, I have a meeting set up with Mr. Carter. "Oh! Oho! Here comes the mission impossible"; my brain was numb for some time. I cursed Rhea if she had not manifested things. I would have been more comfortable for the first meeting. Now it's like entering a Lion's den as dead meat. I took a deep breath and knocked on the door. "Come In", I entered with a small smile on my face and said, "Good morning" to which he didn't even look at me or replied. He just points at the chair directing me to sit. A Late 40's guy in a gray suit, dark specs, and his head delved into his laptop. He then turned to me, "I like people who deliver excellence. Don't keep high hopes of getting promoted soon; people are struggling for years to get into higher positions. You are either very lucky or intelligent enough to out-stand every interview. Let's see how you keep up with your first client. Mr. Robin will be there and can support you with all the details. After this project, you are on your own; handling different clients with their portfolios which will all count in working skills.

My eyes were glued to him while he giving his 'the talk' until there was silence. I didn't realize that I had to leave until he said while snapping his fingers, "What are you waiting for, Christmas!"

"You may leave now and all the wishes."

I just gave thanked him giving a wild smile while escaping from the door, straight to my workspace. I had two glasses of water while taking a short breath. The meeting was way better than I thought.

After a few minutes, we headed to meet a meeting; Mr. Robin holds his grip while handling clients. He is very encouraging while indulging his fellow co-ordinates as well in the discussion which has a healthy outcome with all terms agreed upon. We all were really satisfied with the meeting turning into a crack deal!!

This was a really happy moment. I just wanted to share the things with Rhea. As soon as I entered my cabin, there she was already. I think a birdie informed her; she praised me for my first small success and we decide we go have dinner together. Now, we become like buddies who know each other well now. She helped me a lot through the beginning; so, I felt that I should treat her with dinner as a token of appreciation for her support.

I exclaimed "My treat" and instead of any answer, I got thumbs up with a wild smile. After we left the office, straight reached 'Jin Ramen'. I had visited only this place when I had entered NYC and loved their Asian food, especially their Sushi combos, Crab tempura. So, we settled on Crab tempura, Japanese fried chicken, veggie ramen, and flavored soda to go with it.

We were starving after the hectic long day at work. The attendant served everything that smelled appetizing on the table 'Bon Appetite', Rhea said and we dig into the food. Rhea started discussing some work. She suggested that I need to crack some good clients with Mr. Robin before to start handling the portfolios on my own. Also, I should fetch 1-2 new good portfolios solitarily. I paid the bill with Rhea giving me wild smile after finishing the meal. We were heading to the car. I thanked Rhea for helping me from the start. It's supportive when some stands by your side. Rhea kicked my leg while uttering, "There are no thanks or sorry between friends. Cheers to more...!"

She dropped to my building. I reached my flat, and got into shorts

Sitting on the small balcony; I was in thoughts….

I felt that life is getting back to normal. I was so certain about something in my life now. Being in a corporate job will have life and my rules. I don't know if I want to fall in love but whatever I have with me is making me very satisfied. The night was beautiful and relaxed. I fell asleep as soon as I jumped on my bed.

The following day, we had quarterly meetings which were common although some clients prefer to meet once per month. But I've noticed more success to conduct these meetings through Zoom/Skype as clients just want to understand the future numbers of their business. Consequently, the discussions now happen quarterly. My job as a financial analyst is going to encompass a great deal more than managing investment portfolios or closing sales. It's more of prospecting, marketing, customer service, and compliance that will be part of your daily routine, and your ability to effectively incorporate these tasks into your schedule will ultimately determine your level of success in the business.

Days passed, and a few months passed life was getting into a routine. I was content with my life schedule.

Even if you are on your own, New York is a city that prides itself on offering "everything," As a resident, you can feel overwhelmed by all the choices you have for the fulfillment of your daily needs

And it's true, each day you are bolted up by fierce yellow taxis and hungry subways, only to be emitted back out into their non-stop and spine-tingling city.

My day begins when I sway off the bed and walk the entire length of your apartment to the bathroom with only one swift movement. I continue readying myself for the day, call mom, and get a fix for my caffeine. Sometimes, I do my breakfast at home or grab a bite while hopping into the crowd bustling through the busy streets.

After work as well, you get ready for yourself your voyage home through the hectic traveling, and if you know which car to enter, you avoid the battle.

Over time, the influence of New York City's delightfulness rests on your shoulders, and you appreciate the city of lights, dreams, and opportunity as home. Sometimes I wander through Fifth Avenue, the shopping mall, instead of catching a movie or hitting Broadway. Each night before bed, you understand that you're not simply in existence in the city — you're living it.

"You'll never change your life until you change something. You don't have to be great to start, but you have to start to be great"

Meeting Him!

'You are the love that came without warning,
You had my heart before I could say No...."

So, Rhea suggested that now I should try the nightlife once. I being old school; was an early bed, early rise person. I loved it when I used to be in college, on bike rides, and night strolling. But right now, I like this simple super schedule of mine. Rhea holds a different view. She suggested it was high time I let loose and have some fun. And Rhea never to take 'No' for an answer; we decide to go clubbing. "Drinks, music and dance!" exclaimed Rhea. We will try it out this weekend. She names a few options and finalizes 'Barbarella' which is convenient to get us back home safely after midnight. It was Saturday, and we were thrilled. Day went well; I had to work from home so I just finish a few online meetings and some documentation. After that, I had my lunch which was a simple 'Buddha bowl' and took some rest. By the evening, it was time to get ready; it was the first time I was sitting in front of the cupboard to choose what to wear; Rhea called to tell me that we were taking a cab as the car was at the service station. She said, "I will be at your place and then we can leave from there."

We reached the place, and the pub was fantastic. The ambiance was already making us high! The bang on music, rounds of drinks, and the bodies moving in the air. Rhea, I order some mixed berries martinis, Sangrias, and potato herbed fries. After a few shots, we headed to the dance floor grooving to the tunes of pop and jazz songs. When I was dancing, I suddenly felt that there were eyes that got gloomed on me. When I did see in the same direction, mine got fixed too…

The man was in a jet-black T-shirt and jeans. Simple! yet mesmerizing. His eyes were deep with well-sculpted body, skin pale as moonlight. As this, rounds of staring passed by; there was a silvery glow all around. This was a weirdo fresh feeling. My heartbeat in the stillness of my body was pounding. Control was an illusion right now! A new heartbeat had begun. The stare was distracted by Rhea. She hinted at me to ask him to join us on the dance floor. I take a nervous laugh at the idea and by the time we turn around to look at him again. There was just an empty sit, me looking at Rhea in fuss and Rhea shrugged off her shoulders. Behind came the voice, "Would you mind if I join in?" My mouth got stung at that moment. I was giving him a dumb glance. Rhea helped me out by saying that she will rest and get something to drink, leaving both of us to shake our legs together.

He was bold, "Hi! I'm Kevin!!" Saying that he took my hands in his; then we started moving slowly with tunes. I could have resisted but didn't feel like letting his hand go off. We made some good moves there together. I didn't know how time passed away. It was quite late; I also realize Rhea should get home. Kevin asked if he could drop us off. Rhea suggested that she could take a cab; they can leave directly from here as well. "My home was 7 blocks away so I can get by cab to reach it," Rhea said again looking with a wink.

But I was not a bad friend, so we decide to drop her. While traveling, Rhea was giving so many hints to start the conversations, but I overlooked all. Before she would start with any banter, I requested Kevin to put on some slow music, and then there was silent musical driving in between stares from Kevin. After some time,we reached Rhea's place while wishing us good night she also thanked Kevin for the drive. We left the place; were on the main road steering. I was just gazing outside the window. "Do want to go home, Mr.X?" I was gloomed to the sky. Kevin smiled and said, "Mr.X! I introduced myself but what about you?? "He gave his name but I didn't. I replied, "Mr.X sounds' good right now!!" And yeah! I don't want to go home. I have never behaved like this before. So, Kevin said, "I know just the right place" Kevin was driving for while…

We started a small conversation and asked him about what he does for a living. He was looking at the road, then looked at me and said, he was an amateur model while a part-time cook. In my mind, I thought, "Wow! Good look and a cook…" When I was in my lost in my thoughts, he suddenly stopped the car.

There were all beautiful yachts around. The moonlight was making them shine. He was already out of the car. I followed; he was standing in front of a medium-sized white blue-ish fly-bridge yacht which had two symmetrical leads from this platform to the upper deck. The lower had a cabin with lounge seating for relaxing. He elbowed me while I was taking a glimpse of beauty. He asks over if we could spend some time here. It was his friends' but he had the keys. As the next day was Sunday, I didn't mind at all and couldn't think of anything but just wanted to be with him for now!

He opened the cabin. It was quite furnished. They had a mini fridge as well. He enquired, "Would you like to have something??" I needed some water. He opened the fridge, grabbed a beer for himself, and passed a bottle of water to me. Out of curiosity seeing the fridge so full, I enquired; "Is this fridge always stuffed?" He replied, "Yea! Mostly on weekends my friend rents' the yacht for night outs. I take care of the stuff that. From cleaning to refilling the commodities; "Want to grab a bite?" saying that he checked in for some fruits. While he was chopping them, making dressing for salad; I was alluring his chiseled body. He caught his eye on me and I was a little embarrassed, till then he served the in front of me. This simple dish was quite tempting. I had to compliment him that with such fewer ingredients he created such a sweet dish. While in my thoughts Kevin couldn't resist, he took the spoon and fed me the first bite. I looked at him and opened my mouth.

The spoon was still there and left his hand the spoon, we were staring at each other. "So, how is it?" The spoon fell when I about say "It was deli...." We were just a little close to each other. I was just mesmerized by the current moment. "Was this love at first sight?" I felt shy and moved a little behind. "Let's just stay in I nodded. He took some beer cans in one hand and the other hand in mine and walked towards the deck. Sitting close to each other, he had a beer can in his hand. He handed me one can too. This is close for the first time. I could feel his skin. I was gazing at the sky filled with the star. "Glad you liked it!" I looked in astonishment. He gave the reply to my look with a smirk, "Fruit salad" to which I smiled back. He said he wants to work as a chef in his very own small fancy restaurant. But I don't have enough funding. I liked how he was opening things casually, "Right now, I don't have one, but definitely will treat you one day in mine. I work for small commercials which are enough for savings and keeps life routine going on...!! "And you??" he said. "I'm pretty basic with a 9 to 5 job and travel for work purposes. I call that itself work with pleasure," "Hobbies??" he questioned again. "Traveling to some unique places and trying out different cuisines..." "I could see that!" he sneered while looking at the plate which was half done by me. "What about you?" I questioned. "I like to play guitar. I have one at home. I like to play it for family and friends. I rarely play at stand-up stages when it is proposed by one of my friends. "Wow!" I exclaimed. "You have multi-talents."

While I having a conversation with him, we were finished 1-2 beer cans. The dizziness of the alcohol had started working...

I realized he was directly looking at me. His twinkling blue eyes gave me sweet chills. There was silence, the eyes were talking. Like they wanted something more; with the sudden act he moved forward and kissed my cheeks I didn't even resist; felt like thousand stars twinkling at night. We had a soft smile after the moment. His soft touch on cheeks gave little sparks.

"Maybe it's just infatuation right now or I'm just dreaming", I told myself. Bcoz after a long time someone was so intimated. Like after school and college, when your average bright student you have limited friends who are focused on mark sheets more than having fun. That doesn't mean,

I never enjoyed my company. But studies were more important so fun was limited.

My thoughts suddenly busted when he slowly captured my face. Kevin attacked my lips. In no time, there was rigorous lip lock which I never wanted to get over with…

I felt all new me from the inside but I don't know if my face had those expressions or not. With the reaction on my face, he thought I was least interested. I wasn't sure what Kevin expected but with all my guts I moved in and gave him a cheek peck which he advanced into lip lock again. His silky lips tasted yum and now the bodies were too close, pressing one another. Everything heated up soon; his lips slowly move to the neck. All my thoughts were wobbling in my head which froze as Kevin moved from neck to chest. He unbuttoned the shirt, and I grabbed his hand and straight away looked into his deep eyes, looking at them made me more paralyzed.

He pulled back the hand and then he continued the unwrapping…

When my brain was still on the debate of lust or love? He was already conquering…!! To my conscience, we were still on the deck. Before I could say anything, he pulled; I followed him inside the cabin. On the way, the clothes disappeared as soon as the cabin door was closed. Bodies united, and he pulled me close, his wet lips traveling all over my body leaving goosebumps. The sofa wasn't enough for us.

The floor had become the set out accommodating our bodies. Anchored to each other, the greedy glide continued steaming the temptation. My pulse had already inflamed with ecstasy. Shock waves of pleasure sizzled. Raining kisses all over, rapid and shallow breaths were riding rhythm. Wrestling with his need, throbbing inside me, the touch provoked a cry of unchaining wild, delicious feeling with a shattering climax. He sat down beside and his torso remained visible. There was silence; me holding my breath; enjoying the beauty oozing from Kevin's body. He lay back with his mobile in hand. Me pretending that I had fallen asleep. Knowing that he was staring at me for a while, my eyes were tightly shut. Now he was beside me, I could still his skin against me. The lights were dim and my heartbeat was roaring. He realized, he held me from the back and I could feel my body shaking with uncertainty. He just wanted to know if I'm okay. I don't how much courage I had put to say, "I'm fine"

But, inside my heart was scheming something. I wanted the moment to stand still there…

Everything the light pressure of his hands, the exhales' as they touch my body. I didn't want to escape the harshness of tomorrow's reality. He was the first guy, should he know about it was a real pain in my ass instead of the other as the tiring body had stopped reacting. I let loose his embrace but his hand was still over me. I just moved to the corner. I press my face on my shoulders. I was a little sore, but the pleasurable happiness inside had made it numb already. In college, we try everything from having fun and flirting but I never felt expressive and validated towards those feelings. But tonight, everything made me so brimming with excitement or fantasy, or was it, love??

Whatever it took us to that moment, I'm still fighting with my feelings, I didn't know when I did fall asleep. The next morning, he was already up and dressed and gazing at me. My eyes are half shut, heavy moreover because of the little hangover of last night. I could just see him giving a small smile. He tossed the clothes towards me. I wanted to check whether he was OK after last night but he got ready first. We both had just silent smiles for each other. We clean up the deck and had coffee while getting into the car. Again, had a pure silent smile for each other in the car, only could hear the smooth wind passing by…

He then said, "Sorry you had to hurry down, I have a small meeting for new modeling projects. I don't work on weekends but I had postponed the meeting prior as well due to some reason; had to schedule last minute. Can I drop you somewhere?" Before I could say anything, his mobile buzzed and he was confirming with someone for the meeting. After the call, I replied to him that he could get me a nearby subway, further I will manage. He was ready to drop home, but I refused; I could see he was a little anxious about the meeting. I didn't want to bother him as the meeting felt important to him. The car stopped, and we reached close by the substation. We had a few minutes before going back to routine; just looking into each other eyes. I could feel his flirty and intense eyes. I was sitting there one hand was the door lock of the car and another hand was on my lap which I was above to raise to say "Bye" before that itself his handset rang. It was his casting agent who called him again to confirm and to reach on time; what all talks have to be done with the client, he hinted me to open the door and signal to give me the mobile number while he was still on the mobile phone. That half-done goodbye was more irritating. I close the door, and took you few steps forward; I received a call from mom which went on for another 10 min. I waved at Kevin while I was on and he did the same. When the call ended, I took a few steps forward with a sudden realization that we forgot to exchange numbers or any contact details I rapidly turned around, to see that he must still be there; but all in vain as the car was already off my sight. I was standing there just covered with terrible sad feelings and didn't want to move. My mobile buzzed again, Rhea was on the line, who called to check in if I was back home and done with a hangover, she forced me in for lunch but I suggested indoors, she finally fixed the thing saying that she brings lunch as she came to my residence. I just say yes and kept the call; hurried up and reached home. For a while, I lay on my bed. And my mind started playing games. I pushed myself to have a bath.

"Ahh! Did he like it or not?" "Was it only lust!" "What about the feelings which were true and deep, we could see that in each other's eyes" All thoughts were wandering in my mind. "Was it destined this way..." One night??" "Kevin!" I yelled as notions were floating under the shower in my head. Got dressed up and was about to sit on the sofa, but the doorbell rang. I was a little surprised when Mrs. Roy was there with some cookies box in hand. She was there just to have coffee together as had not met for a couple of weeks. I told her that we partied yesterday and were not back home. I stayed at a friend's place. I did ask about her school counseling. She then enquired about the lunch plans. I told Rhea was coming over as it was Sunday, I asked Mrs. Roy to join in, as I too wanted to be distracted...

So, I guess it was a small pot lunch buffet for us. My mind was concentrated on Kevin. Mrs. Roy said that she will prepare something and get upstairs till Rhea comes in. She insisted and I couldn't deny it. You will never feel alone when good friends are around and become your emotional support indirectly. By the time I complete my work and surf Netflix in between. The doorbell rang again. Rhea was at the door with lunch I invited her in after seeing the apartment. She had been 1-2 times before, but she just picked me up, except for this one time she wanted me to get settled in starting days at work where she had been only for 10-15 min. But today she wanted to overlook around and everywhere. I handed her a glass of water. While us talking about projects fund management for some clients, sitting on my apartment's balcony which is now my favoritecozy corner. It is spacious enough to fit in a couple of chairs and a coffee table, as we had kept the door half open, Mrs.Roy entered the room, and I introduce both of them. They got together in an instant, talking to each other like BFFs.

Mrs. Roy had prepared some old-style gnocchi with some custard. Rhea brought mushroom vegetable cheese pie. And a good big tub of ice cream while I was a little embarrassed that it was my home, I should play the role of entertaining the guest, but it was the reverse. Luckily, there was some drinking stuff in the fridge... I open the fridge; hand orange juice, wine, and beer cans to Rhea. We then start plating. Rhea and Mrs.Roy were chirping around and also cleaned my room as I woke late and didn't check my room. Otherwise, I'm a tidy person. Well, at conversation Rhea heard that I was not home last, and she raised an eyebrow. I know she wanted to know every detail but I glance at her and told her to shut up with my eyes. While eating, the three of us were having casual talks and gave each other updates about what happened over the last couple of weeks. After the meal, Rhea and I cleaned the plates. We were about to have ice cream when Mrs.Roy gets a call from her colleague to discuss some sessions. She keeps the call by saying that she will call back in another 10-15min then finalize. "Don't forget to keep me a scoop of ice cream" she said and left with a smiley face.

I close the door. Rhea was sitting like a crouching tiger waiting for prey. She attacked me to let out every detail... I told her the whole night was amazing but I did not want this day to start like that. We fail to remember exchanging numbers. She laughed but then seeing my antagonism she felt pitiful. Suddenly she got up to pull my cheeks for cheering me up. "We can find a way out to reach him on social media" with that she closes tub of ice cream. I hoped to work this way out. Everything happy moment comes with a time limit, I guess!" You can't have the same feeling for 24 hours; I felt the part of me left with Kevin. I was thinking will he have the same feeling, is he also missing me?! And was this love? If not, then this agony will not remain for long!!"

Rhea brought me back from the thoughts by touching the ice cream tub on my cheek and handing it to me to keep in the refrigerator. Now, there is just a tingling feeling called 'hope' inside me. I needed the topic to change then Rhea reminded me about the meeting for the upcoming projects. We discussed the same for some time. She said that she will pick me up before the meeting. And we can brief things again in the morning for the upcoming projects. She picked up the next morning while we discussed the same. As a consultant, I have to work on projects which make our company a familiar name in the industry so that we became a brand. I brought my focus to work. Big clients are coming and we make more profit. That is the best thing I like about 'Silverman & Co', they focus on both company and individual growth. I want to work hard for the same. Each project success ratio is a step to building personal growth as well. We had selected a few clients for taking up big projects. The meeting continued for 3 hours, ideas were flooding in, debates, and then finalizing the team to work for the same. I and Rhea headed for lunch. We were supposed to sit in the company's cafeteria but as we had no meeting further. Only, I had a small discussion with the CEO in the evening around 4.30 pm. We decide to drop in the nearby bistro. Rhea drove the car. I was engrossed in an article by "The Financial Diet". It's important to Budget your money is important; that's one good thing dad taught me. So, you have an easy life after the age of retirement. I consider the same, there will house and relaxing chair in front of it having drink in one hand. Rhea pinched me which brought me to reality. We were at Orchid's where we order some pink pasta, salad, and chocolate-filled croissants. Rhea after taking a few morsels said she tried searching for the name Kevin but didn't have any luck in finding the right one; or if we could have the last name or some other hint. I don't remember anything except for his cooking skills and the glow on his face while we were under the starry sky. I acted like I was trying to recollect, but all in vain. The only thing my mind started thinking about was his touch and cuddles and all moments of that night reoccurred in my mind. Arrgh! I hate Rhea for doing this to me. Clenching heartbroken, I was just holding my emotions back. I gently rubbed the temple of my head and ask Rhea to stop the subject. "What happened was enough for me to survive". Now, I know what is wanted by me and maybe he is the only one I wanted to be with me. But destiny didn't accept that, it is now our choice of how to survive the same. If it was everything will fall into place. It's not like he cheated, we are both loyal to those moments, I could feel that in his eyes. Rhea called for 'Bill'

It was an unsaid deal between Rhea and me that we pay alternatively. Rhea tapped my shoulder and said; "To hold on and hope will bring on the light despite all darkness."

We left the restaurant and drove back to the office. The meeting was smooth. It was an introductory meeting with the CEO; so, Rhea was also there. He congratulated me on getting good projects and we discuss future business plans. It was thought to have a such session at the start of the career in the company. We had a good brain-storming session with him. After, the meeting was done. I headed towards the Subway to get home. I already told Rhea that I wanted to go alone today. I wanted to catch my breath back and get over everything. A small walk to my building from the subway would revive me. I reached home and threw my bag on the sofa. I didn't know what this feeling was but felt empty. As nothing was left there in the heart; Love?? I was just questioning myself and wandering in my thoughts. But where and who will solve this puzzle? As techno-savvy, the dumbest thing I could do which I did was googled; "Did you fall in love online test!" Now, this may be crazier, but I answered a few questions and the result was positive! LOL! This was making me more confused about the feelings I have right now! I felt that just wanted to meet him once so that I could at least understand his love. Love at first sight?? Really?

Later had my dinner, did the dishes, and was back on my bed. I don't know but today I felt like listening to some soft song, 'Where is my love.' by SYML got stuck in my mind and I played it the same until I was snoring the night away. The next morning, we had a few meetings and it was very packed with a lot of work. I was in the office focused on Mr. Shawn's meeting file. There was investment management for upcoming projects which needed a final go-through. Some more office stuff, some clerical work was going on and on…

Days passed by; I was too involved in my work. We were hopping toward many new projects. There were different teams, budget planning, and making reports. Everything, every day was perfectly going on. But void still with hope that we will meet at a U-turn was at the back of my mind. At home, mom calls would be relief bursts. I could talk to her about work, and life going on here. Whenever I was free, used to visit the nearby famous place and Rhea introduced me to some friends as well. So, sometimes the weekend was fun.

During lunch, Rhea asked me if I was free on Sunday, so she wanted me to meet her friend. I know where this was heading; but didn't want to discuss it. I was trying to find an excuse but before I say anything Rhea insisted, "Look, I understand deep down you are anguished but try to get over it. Think of it as one night experience. I know it's insensitive to say this but you can take it as practice lessons" she said that while smirking. I was furious by those words but her smirk had just me give her a lunatic smile. I just nodded in agreement. She smiled back as she was content to get 'YES' as an answer. I felt blessed, as she was trying to get the broken heart back to normal…

"Letting go is hard but being free is beautiful. Positive anything is better than negative nothing."

On- Offs…

Turn off your brain and turn on your heart!
You can't turn 'LOVE' ON and OFF like faucet…

I realized that we were not destined as I tried to check in the bar once or twice but all in vain…

Here Rhea had already started to find new ways to get my social life back as I was becoming more workaholic. True friends will bother and irritate you for good. So, I decided that we will go out for dinner together which made Rhea smile as well as I was content with my heart to start fresh. But, we have also that one friend who comes with surprise packages. You never know 'what is next store' in for you when you're with that friend. And Rhea was a super package of all…

When she parked the car, she did an unexpected announcement that she has invited 'Alex' as well. I gave her an irritated look so she could inform me prior that we are going to have a strange guest along. Before I could say anything,

Rhea was already out of the car waving at the person. I couldn't think of any backup plan right now as I was very hungry and the so-called 'Alex' was already parking his black Lyan Lykan Hypersport. It's very impressive that he owns this turbocharged engine. He parked it near the restaurant. Rhea picked me up from staring from inside the car. She gave a signal to come out and gave a cheerful smile while walking toward Alex. Wow! Perfect body-hugging Polo shirt with Denim He came nearby, hugged Rhea with "Long time no see, they just started chit chat. I wanted to disappear for a moment. Not that he was good-looking. He was substantially gorgeous and will be adored by girls. But right now, food was on my mind as hunger had reached a super level. Rhea called my name and broke my thoughts. She introduced me and Alex. Rhea had already reserved a table. We started with wine and starters. Alex was giving the same stare Kevin had given the first we met. I gave him well-mannered smile. Rhea was about to say something but her phone buzzed; she excused herself eyeing me to start the conversation while she started walking to the hotel veranda to attend to her call.

There was an awkward silence at the table. To break the glass, I asked Alex how he knows Rhea; to which Alex said that they both had done some PG program together. And thereafter we stayed in touch even when the program was completed as we enjoyed each other's company. Rhea completed her call and joined us again. To my relief, we had small talks and other conversations. We finished our meal, and Alex insisted on paying the bill to which Rhea cheerfully agreed. I just was glad the meet-up was over. We reached the gate. Thankfully, Rhea got the car, good that we parting ways soon. I not complaining but it was too fast to handle things. Alex suddenly asked for my number while Rhea got the car nearby. I looked at him, gave him small smile, and just said "Sure!"

Rhea drove me back home, I was still frowning but she brought the ice cream tub out, smiling said, "Sorrrrrry!" almost melting my irritation. She alleged that you would find an excuse if you told beforehand. We didn't argue further on this and started watching some episodes of web series digging in the tub of ice cream. After Rhea left watching a few episodes, I was sitting isolated on the bed, the thoughts made clouds around me. I realize at some point I will have to move on…

My ice cream tub was empty; I went to the kitchen and place it on the platform. Coming back to the bedroom, played "Apologies" by Timbaland. I wanted my mind to calm down so I can think right to take some right steps. Was sitting bedroom balcony, gazing at the sky; really what went wrong? I thought to myself. I was missing his touch. Is it even possible? I don't know how to move forward. Should I take my chances? Do I know what I want now?? Well, I guess time is the best healer with that thought; I jumped on the bed.

The next morning, I felt fresh. By the balcony, I took little light wind on my face. There were three meetings lined up, had no time in between. Other tasks to be completed were reviewing client portfolios, answering client inquiries, and addressing outstanding issues. While the two meetings were done, it was lunch break. I came close to Rhea's cabin and gave her a smile which was understood by her that I will try. I could not do much of the talking as I was heading out for my 3rd meeting. With that, it will end the day. I decide to go home directly and informed Rhea about the same. While I was near the elevator, Mrs. Roy was coming down. She asked me about work and other stuff. While we were talking, she enquired if I needed anything from groceries. I was free after work, done with laundry yesterday itself, I didn't want to go home so early. I asked Mrs. Roy if she cared I join her in...

Giving smile she said, "OH! Not all!"; "In fact, I will get you introduced to 2-3 local shops which have nice discounts on regular groceries, daily essentials, fruits, and vegetables. Let's walk…"

I loved the small talks in between while I was enjoying the silence of my mind. Of course, there were car honks, people crisscrossing, small shop vendors, children playing in the park, and smell from local coffee shops after a long time everything was revitalizing. Sometimes the winters can become shitty but very few days out of the blues are less chilly; the breeze is quite soothing. We reached nearby Costco and did get some deals on groceries. While coming home we took a cab as there were bags to handle and it would again be a 15-20 min walk. Reached home, and after a long time Mrs. Roy had dinner with me. She had already done some meal prep which real common these days and is time-saving as well. Whenever you're starving, either toss or reheat the food. She had prepared some fried rice, skin braised tofu with some greens to go with it. We had a good dinner.

I was about to take leave for my flat, thanking her for the meal I insisted that she plans one dinner at my house. I will cook and we can chit-chat. You can also meet my friend Rhea, who is my co-worker as well.

Just another day with a lot of commitments, and I was much happier with the outcome. I could get a few new client portfolios which added more perks to my current working grades. The seniors around were pleased with the small progress. I was somewhat satisfied with my status right now. Single, handsome, and hardworking! My smile was at its stretch…

Rhea poked my thoughts; it was time for lunch. We headed to a local restaurant nearby. Rhea already had guessed that Alex and I have already started texting each other. To stop her from the topic, I asked her about my progress, and what I can do to make more to stretch my vision. Thank God! It worked. I distracted her. We were done with lunch. I was supposed to leave from here for my new client. The meeting was set up in his office. Rhea said it was on the way to our office so you are getting a free drive. Rhea was driving the car; she was already ready to roll out the questionnaire from my current status with Alex. Before that I shut her up, saying this is your punishment for keeping me uninformed about the guest appearance of Alex for the meal that day. So, you will never get any bytes of conversation. Rhea gave me a vicious smile; I narrowed my smile and turned to open the door of the car as already reached my destination. Rhea started the engine again, leaving for work. She dropped one nastier smile with a challenge that she will find out everything; with me teasing her with her tongue out, while saying goodbye. Before leaving, she informed me that she will be out of town for some personal reasons…

After a client meeting, I headed home; made some coffee for myself, sat with my laptop started working on my presentations, working on finances you need an update about the current business status, and the market altercation. Reading some online financial journals while completing my project presentations; I didn't know how time passed by...

While it was dinner time; I was not yet starving so decided to clean my wardrobe a bit, ordering some food delivery I prepared my clothes for tomorrow. While I was in the middle of doingall this; I get a ping, to my surprise or not it was Alex

Alex: Hey! Are u free?

I had no idea what to reply hence went with the flow...

Me: Yea! Say??

Alex: Can we meet again?? Whenever you Ok with??

Maybe dinner or going to the pub?

I didn't want to sound impolite now, but currently, my work was my focus more on career goals to achieve, hold my position firm, and move ahead to a bright luxurious future. Therefore, goes my lousy reply.

Me: Maybe next weekend.

The doorbell rang. My food arrived, plunging into some vegetable chili in burnt garlic sauce, fried wanton and marinated tofu with broccoli.

There was another ping on my mobile which I ignored; I served my dinner at 8.30 pm which is

my usual dinner time these days. Weekends can go to any time, Rhea in sync will make me go partying or we binge-watch some web series or football match. I switch to Netflix. I heard one more ping on my mobile. I was sure it was not Rhea as she is out of town for some personal work. It was an unsaid rule that we are not supposed to buzz each other. We can catch up on everything as we meet the very next. I thought it would be Mr. Robin to brief me about Friday's meeting. To my surprise, it was Alex again suggesting a video call. I was still not comfortable. I replied that I was having food; will call him tomorrow late evening to which he pinged OK with smile emoji. That's a relief!

I made a random call to mom. She had won some society awards for her small social work. She occupied higher education but after marriage, she dedicated her life to being at home doing the duties of wife and mother. But the one thing she by no means gave up was lending a hand to others. That only thing my father never opposed for. She usually arranges food bequests in festivals, blood donations, and education programs. She believed small initiatives can make a little bigger difference.

She was happy to hear my voice. The community has a small gathering for her appreciation. She enquired about what food I eat, work and health. I guess it's with all moms; they feel if their kids don't have home food. They will starve to death. I informed her that I have an Indian community around then enquired about dad. He is yet not talking to me as I rejected a few more girls. He feels that I'm losing all good opportunities. Mom enquired about Rhea as she is well-updated with my daily routine here and the people around her. We had a very long conversation today; I started yawning in between. Before keeping the cell phone, conveyed to mom to come here to stay with me for some time. She refused saying that getsomeone first, will be to meet your loved one…!!

With cheesy lines and smiles, we ended the call.

The next day was smooth, the client was happy with my presentation on financial analysis for their upcoming project. Rhea was supposed to resume work after 2 days. I thought she would be in her cabin. To my surprise, she was not;

called her but no response. I wanted to order food for lunch; except needed some fresh air after heavy discussion, went to grab a subway with a fruit drink

Got a text from Mrs. Roy enquiring if I can visit for dinner after work? While I was nibbling, confirmed her with the last bite in my mouth. I had one meeting to attend with 2-3 reports to be updated. My work got over a little early today, so thought of grabbing some stuff from the local market for myself and Mrs. Roy.

After a while, I reached home and kept my stuff. Came down to Mrs. Roy's floor and rang the bell. Astonished when Rhea opened the door; I asked her about what is she doing there while entering the living room. "How did you get here??" was the first query shot by me. Rhea gave a wild smirk, "I was stalking you…"

"Yeah, right! Whatever!!" I started walking to the kitchen near the dining table to see Mrs. Roy and Rhea followed. "How was your day?" Mrs. Roy enquired. I was talking about work. I gave a small intro to Rhea as well. After having a delicious meal, we played 2-3 rounds of cards, "I won again" Mrs. Roy exclaimed. I made a puffy face. She perfectly knew what I wanted whenever gloomy expressions were made by me.

The candy jar was a stress buster. By now, I knew a few symbol predictions, but this time I received a purple jelly bird. Rhea received a heart shape toffee. She raised her eyebrow with twinkling eyes as Mrs. Roy gave her a 'be in love with' hint. For me, bird means freedom; as well as optimism and joy. Maybe you will find passive solutions for your problems with which

I hopefully smiled back at her. I guess, we both knew that I wanted to hear something like that...

We bid good night to her and came down. Rhea had parked the car a few blocks away. We could walk; as I took a few steps it felt refreshing. The night puff of air was restful. Rhea was right! You should at least try changing something around. You don't have to live a monotonous life. Rhea cleared her throat which brought me back from my thoughts. She was looking at me with a raised eyebrow, waiting for some response. Finally, accepting my defeat, I gave her a small grin. "So, it's a work in progress", she said while smiling back at me. Rhea didn't want to invade further but she knew that I might give Alex a chance. Without saying anything, I wished her again good night as we came near the car.

The next few days were smooth. The client was happy with the presentation, and financial analysis for the project. Rhea resumed work after a mini vacation. There was a lot of work in our department so we could not even have lunch together. We met after work. I ordered some food for lunch, also prepared reports, and explored investment opportunities for the project. Evaluating some profit plans as well. Mrs.Roy texted me enquiring if I can visit her after work, I confirmed the same with the last chunk of meal in my mouth. After that, I scrutinize and sampled some of the projects. I get a random ping from Rhea as a gentle reminder to callback Alex for a meeting at the weekend which I entirely forgot. "What are the sources of your childish prattles? I texted back with wink emoji; but got a reply "It's secret" with mock emoji which was not, in the case. Alex must have called…

I replied "Ok" with a smile. Back to work, I put my head into my laptop with a happy mind thinking of the current career graph until Mr. Robin came into my cabin, he was there for taking a glimpse at past projects. He is a really good chap, very helpful, and even scolded me for my impractical mistakes while managing some of the accounts. We were discussing a lot of stuff. In end came the real shock that I will be on my own for the next project. I will be having 2 assistants under me like Mr. Robin; the decision-making authority on projects will be under my control. Mr. Robin was waiting for my reaction. I could barely smile but I was glad that me being one step closer to my goal. Robincongratulated me; giving best wishes for the future he stood up to leave my cabin. Coming to my sense, we did a handshake. He said, "Even though the pace is unhurried it's good enough. Don't worry; we will always be supporting each other. I thanked him for giving such delightful news, and with a big smile on my face started working on my laptop. I wanted to call mom, but thought to make it for the weekend so that chat for a long…

Left a little early today, and plan to do some grocery shopping for the weekend; as I wanted to celebrate it with Mrs.Roy and Rhea by cooking for them. Some rich wine, spaghetti with grilled veggies beer. Some frozen snacks as well; I'm sure; will not be able to make a lot of stuff at the same time. Done with shopping, came to my habitat. Got refreshed and stored the stuff which I brought just now. The mobile buzzed, and Mrs. Roy called to come down. I left some stuff on the dinner table, took my key, and came downstairs. She welcomed me with a few pieces of sliced apples. "How was the day??" "Was something urgent??" I enquired while texting Rhea about the good news I received in the morning.

"No! I just wanted to know if your free this coming 14th Feb on Valentine's", she replied. I raised my eyebrow while she gave me wicked smile and said, "You got to run with me" she gave wild laugh and said, "It's supposed to be for charity which is organized by one of the NGOs which she often visits. The prize for this run is $20,000 but that is deduced to be donated. But that's not it! There is something more stored in it. It is a couple pass to this expensive beachside resort with one yacht ride to watch the sunset on the river Mississippi. All I could hear was the word 'yacht' with all flashbacks coming towards me. The unsaid things wandering in my mind started wobbling. The thought of Kevin made me smile and be gloomy at the same time. Aunty Roy snapped back from the memories. We decide that will take part in the run as it was for good cause. I asked Mrs. Roy to let Rhea join in as well. "The more the merrier" Mrs. Roy exclaimed. She explained that now how we need to create a schedule; practice at least for an hour for the run. Also, maintain a good diet for some days. "Roger that! Captain", I replied as above to take a leave from Mrs. Roy's house. My phone rang, it was Alex! I was above to disconnect the call. Don't know whatchanged my mind; I picked up the call, "Alex Hi! How are you? It's been a while…!! So, what's up??

Alex replied, "Hi, I'm fine. Work is a little hectic. We have a couple of strong projects," and then there was some silence.

"Hello", Yea! Yea! I'm there on the call. It's just that I wanted to ask you something, "OK, shoot!! What is it?? Are you ok?" I instantly followed up to which Alex replied with a smile. I could see through the cell phone that he was happy that I was concerned about him. He then asked, "Can we go on date this Valentine's?"

"Just me and you" "Only if you're comfy with it" There was a small awkward silence. "Hello!" Alex said "I'm there"

"Sorry, the thing is I just promised to volunteer in a charity run to support an NGO. And the event is on Feb14th. So??"

Alex replied, "No problem, we meet late or I can join in?? Is that possible? It would be quite a different kind of rendezvous…"

"We can spend the whole day together after that…"

I signaled Mrs. Roy; with a smile, she nodded 'Yes'. I replied to Alex, "Alex, I will send you other details in a while, we can plan accordingly. "Is that OK?"

"Yeah", replied Alex. With a wishing good night, we closed the call. Before leaving Mrs.Roy asked if she should be called Rhea to which I replied, "No, I will inform her about the event tomorrow in the office; reaching my apartment, and sitting on the sofa. I was just thinking about what happened. I'm guessing, 'time is healing everything' The better option was to give it a chance to yourself or 're-love'; laid on my bed reading 'Freakonomics' by Steven D. Levitt and Stephen J. Dubner and didn't know when did I doze off.

The next day we started with some meetings and presentations. Later half we had a new client in for its first meeting. He was some big shot. Our colleagues had a small group discussion about the same. We needed some big portfolios on our list. Our company already had a few A+ clients but we wanted some big names to add in; to be prominent in the market. After little debating, itwas decided that everyone has the chance to make their presentations. Whoever does their best will get this portfolio. I was the one least interested, as I already was packed with few good clients, so already putting my hands off the project.

Rhea was waiting for me at the gate. I got into the car and promised her dinner. We entered one of our favorite spots 'TAO downtown' which was one best spots for Asian food. We order a crispy Bao bun with pad Thai noodles. The drinks came first.

"So, what's your plan for Valentine's?" I asked. Rhea's eyes popped out with a question. "Chillax" "I had to just know if you're busy; I would not let the plan ruin because I have decided to go for a charity run for an NGO group which Mrs. Roy is working for... "Rhea responded, "As if you don't know. We both are singles; I was going to pal a movie night but this sounds much better…" "And it's not just us", I riposted.

As usual, her eyebrow rose to the corner of her forehead. She was excited when I told her that I have asked Alex to join in for the event. She suggested that after the run you should invite him home, have lunch together or plan something for the rest of day; you get more time with each other. I was listening like she was a cupid max level pro while I'm an amateur lover. She was by now hunting some romantic date ideas on the internet. She was a total 'enthu-cutlet' when it came to matchmaking. "We have 2-3 days, so let's plan something nice," said Rhea with a wicked smile while I was taking another bite. We did the paycheck. I wanted to walk, so insisted Rhea take leave first. I stroll around. I started walking to the nearest subway.The night was picturesque. Walking on a moonlit night not only removes the tiredness and boredom of the chaotic day but also lifts the spirit, enlivens the soul, and refreshes the mind.

Moreover, the cool air kisses each object of nature, presenting a charming sight. One feels an inexplicable sense of thrill and joy. There comes the freedom of mind, thoughts, and ideas.I thought maybe this was right!! Sometimes, life takes a lot of twists and turns, ups-downs. I was relaxed. Maybe, I needed a change. Everything will come on track in while.

Where I was today, I didn't even feel that I could make it till here…

Sometimes, you have to just let it go. Life will let you learn your lesson one at a time. I took the subway and reached home. My eyes were already heavy; I changed into my favorite black shorts and was on my bed in no time. After these 2 client projects and events, I will take some days off for vacation as I revitalized myself again. The rest two 2-3 days went too fast or rather I was indulging in work so much didn't know the period pass by.

Finally, the 'day of Love' came. I was already up, getting dressed. Prepared glass noodles salad. I'm becoming slowly a 'Pro' in cooking; had a moment of pride for myself. I was not hungry so packed it for later after the run. Sure thing! Rhea will need it. I called up Mrs. Roy to check whether she was ready. Called her up, and she replied that she had already done her errands. But she will leave before because at the venue; she had some arrangements to be taken care of. I didn't want to wait. I was excited about this run, I insisted I will come along and can be a helping hand too…

I called Rhea to check if she was ready. She confirmed that she will pick up Alex and meet us at the event directly. Mrs.Roy and I reached the venue first. I volunteer for back stages work, 'to check the water counter', and 'checking the badge counter. Then, I called Rhea to ensure that they reach in time to which she replies that they will be there in another 10-15 minutes. She requested to register the names as well…

"Oh Yeah!" I missed it, will do it now saying that I kept the handset. I register Alex and Rhea's names for the run. They gave us badge numbers. Mrs.Roy wished me luck while she took care of the medical aid counter. Rhea, Alex reached. I handed them the badges. Alex spoke, "Hi, how are you? All the best wishes…" I smiled at that, he said "After the run, we can have lunch together, I know a place where we can head later" I looked at him. He was too spontaneous; his hair was styled; blue shirt and shorts were looking good on him. I replied to him, "Yeah, we can have lunch together. Best wishes to you as well!"

We all were at the crease; "Get, set, Go!!" there was a roar and everyone started a slow run. I loved the spirit of the people around me. Every person working for a good cause; somehow, I didn't know we lost track of each other. Rhea was ahead, I guess. There was a vast crowd. Alexwas around me but then we both took a little speed.

After a while I was looking around for both of them, suddenly I tripped, and I bruised my knee. Out of the crowd, there came a hand with a voice; "Hey! Hold my hand; let's go aside on the first aid counter. I didn't even look up but held the hand. He didn't leave my hand until the band-aid was done. I was so concentrated on the wound, with the realization that my hand was still in the grip of someone. I turn face up; I couldn't believe it; "Kevin! It is my Kevin." I don't how there was an emphasis on the word 'my' in mind. I lost words. Kevin was way too stunned by the moment. He just pulled me closer and hugged me so tight as if never wanted me to leave…

I came to my senses, and the only thing that came to my mind was annoyance; I felt he hoodwinked me. I couldn't control myself and punched his face. It was light but left mark on his pink skin. He was too shocked with his reaction but hold my hand again. Out of nowhere came Rhea with Alex who thought some misdemeanors were happening; without thinking he sprang on Kevin.

I had to come in between to stop all chaos!! Rhea kept a hold on Alex. Kevin was not ready to leave my hand. I furiously looked at him and asked him to wait for a few seconds. He was still not ready to leave my hand. I explained to Rhea what happened and told her that I'm taking Kevin to my home. There is a lot of unspoken stuff…

Rhea said, "You can take the car", to which Kevin replied, "It's ok. I have my car. I can drop him off after we talk. I could just give a glare.

Rhea to cut off drama left first from the event. Alex didn't take any of it well; I could know by his looks. But he preferred to go with Rhea. Kevin, on the other hand, was very stubborn to get me to his maroon Versa. We didn't care about the race anymore and everyone disappeared from the event; I texted Mrs.Roy that we had to leave early due to an urgent situation. Also assured her that there is nothing to worry about…

I was sitting beside Kevin on the front sit in the car. Kevin was looking at me and then at road. I was intently looking at window, Kevin roared the engine. The car was on the main street now. There was a silence for another 15-20 min. He suddenly stops the car in the middle of the road.

I panicked when car honked from behind. I looked at him astonished; screamed at him. "Plz! God Sake, just take car at one side Kevin" He did as told without speaking a word; came out of car, pulled my side door and took me out the car. I never behaved like this but I don't know what got it me; I did hit his chest, screaming, "Why did you this to me. Just Why??" He pulled me closer, our torso combined. He is little tall then me which was an advantage for him. He looked down at him, bends his face a litter; our lips are an inch away from each other. He gently pressed his lips on mine; we continued the same hunger until Kevin's hands started working their way inside my T-shirt, I quickly moved back while he gave me a wild grin.

"I…" before I could say anything Kevin cut me off, "Can we go somewhere, eat and then talk." I let out a small laugh, "Yes we could do that…" I requested him to come home. We got in the car, Kevin holding my hand. I kept the keys on the table. I signaled Kevin and told him to remove the shoes. I was a little germ freak. He came inside the living room after me. He hugged me from behind. I pushed him again lightly. I was still mad at him, "Why did you not try to get in touch with me?" "At least I tried to find you; I went to the bar again to check!" "Was it just casual sex?" "If that is the thing, please we will part away right now" I just wanted to meet one more to clear things up…!" I bickered. He was staring at me with hiding his smile. I was irritated when he got up from the seat and came close to me. "What do you think I didn't try?" "In that case, you had a name. "What was Isupposed to say at the bar when I went to look for you?"

"Find me Mr.X?" Kevin replied.

I remembered, being playful at that time. I never mentioned my name to him. He was looking at me with a mischievous smile. "Clearly, I'm not the one at fault. Sooo, can I punish you now?" saying that he pulled me closer; attacking my neck with love bites. I could not resist but follow his moves, we plunged onto the sofa. "Rohan," I said releasing the lip lock. "Huh," Kevin reacted. "My name is Rohan" He smiled at me.

"Now, please get up. Let's have some food", I got up and dragged Kevin with my hand. We were at my small dining table and both were starving. I instantly prepared open facesandwich, some fries, and some cold coffee. As we sat at the table,

Kevin dived into a plate from fries to large bites of sandwiches. "This is good," he said with a mouthful of fries. I chuckled at his childish act. I was just contented to see him again. While he was occupied with eating, I admired Kevin's smile, his deep blue eyes, and the naughtiness in his actions. Maybe I have started falling for him.

After completing the meal, Kevin helped me in doing the dishes. I refuse to take help from him but he denied my request and I took his offer; he will make the popcorn while we decide to watch some good movies together.

I was on the couch surfing to put something fun, he came with a bowl of popcorn and sat beside me keeping his head on my shoulder. I had butterflies in my stomach. "What kind of movie do you want to watch?" I asked Kevin. "I like all genres. But mostly action and romcoms are my favorites" "We can watch 'Two-week notice,' said Kevin. I said, "Ok" and we started watching the movie. We were halfway through the movie and Kevin moved closer to give me a slow neck peck to which my response was a mini moan. He locks into his arms and moves his face right in front of my face. I looked into his profound blue eyes; frozen in his arms. The eyes were doing the talk. We didn't need words; looking at the smile on each other's faces was simply satisfying.

"I have to go..." Kevin said with cheerless eyes. I hugged back closer. He gave a little laugh. "Dumbo" he smacks on the head. "I have an outdoor photo shoot for a clothing brand but only for 2 days. Let's go for a date after I come or we can go for a weekend trip away from all that noise, hustle and bustle that can become draining. I don't want just a dinner date. Either it can be in Hampton or Lake Sebago. Luckily, the city that never sleeps is surrounded by sandy beaches; mountain vistas; and sparkling lakes – that make it easy to decompress. You decide to take a bus, train, or drive a car; most of these vivid spots are within easy reach of New York City."

"Hello! Earth to Rohan", he snapped. I was still in my thoughts amazingly looking at him. "Is it too fast for you? Shall we take things at a slow pace?"

"No" "Are you crazy?" "I just don't have words to express my feelings right now but I too wantspent time with you, and know you more. I want to understand your likes and dislikes. I'm captivated by this moment. Am I daydreaming?"

He pinched my cheeks, "No" he retorted. "I know we are still unfamiliar with each other. I'm not even considering a steady connection! But, I felt the spark when we first met. I still remember the day at the bar, the night spent at the yacht" "I felt the liking for you is genuine and loyal"

"Okay okay! Stop!" I felt embarrassed as if he was confessing. "I put forward that let's go with the flow. Each one's connection pace is different; there's nothing wrong with slowing down a relationship, we are not putting labels here, are we? So, we are on the same page!" I nodded.

"Roger that Sir!", "so in between casual and serious" he said that with a wink. "I have already stored my number in your phone" while saying that he got ready to leave. "How did you manage?' He explained that I had called someone and left the phone unlocked for a moment. So, you have the number. "Don't you dare go out of touch!" with that he kissed my forehead. I have started cherishing his small gestures. At the door, he kissed me again on the cheeks. Promise me that we are going trip. Let's have a fresh start on our relationship with this trip. Bye!" "Hmm", and kissed him back on his cheeks.

I close the door, the smile was so obvious, I felt my cheeks blazing. I started cleaning the room, took shower as I was exhausted, and retired to bed. After a very long time, I had sound sleep.

The next morning, I woke up niggling tone of my cell phone. "Where the hell were you? Are you mad? You didn't text me at night about your safety. Are you ok? Are you still with Kevin?" Please talk about something?" Rhea babbled. "Take some breaths in between while talking, Ms. Rhea" I gave silly laugh to which Rhea I'm sure gave a wild smirk. "Someone is quite happy and cheerful!" "All details now!" she demanded. I said let me get fresh, we will meet directly in the office." C'mon now! But you owe me a big treat!" with that she kept the phone. I was on the bed, thinking about yesterday. "Why life plays such games? I wanted to move on but then now I want to move on only with Kevin, he has just captured me from day one. We had this minute error that got clear. I feel that everything falls into place at the right time. I thank Rhea for being such support whileAlex; Oh! Shit, Alex! I exclaimed and feared what would be his response. I should clear out things up with Alex; I don't want to have any wrong ideas. I forgot to ask Rhea about him. So, the first thing I need clear things up with is Alex, and the next share my happy news with Rhea and Mrs.Roy...And finally, plan everything for the weekend trip. 'Whoo- hoo!

I'm getting crazy' with that I got off my bed, bathed, and before leaving the bedroom I made it tidy.

I was in the kitchen and made some coffee for myself. While I was about to make pancakes, my phone beeped, it was a text msg. Then there was one more beep. I made the batter three and kept it aside; picked up my phone and opened the text message. It brought a small smile as it said, "Good morning, Rohan! I just left for my shoot, missing you already. Are you already off from work? The next one was "When I will back, I want to meet you for dinner? Also, Can I choose a place for a trip and you decide how to spend the day? The best thing was he saved his number under the name 'Mr. X's Lover' I texted him back, "Good morning, Kev! Best Wishes for photo-shoot. Yes! And we meet soon."

After a while, I was done with my breakfast, clean my kitchen, and make sure everything was shut before leaving the living room. I texted Mrs.Roy, "Dinner is on me today; will be coming early." I got a reply, "What's the news?" Can she read my mind; I was saying that in my mind. "Nothing much, I wanted to have dinner with you today?"

"Okay, meet you at dinner" I got another text. While traveling, I was thinking about Alex, as I have toamend my muddle while I might hurt his emotion. Once, I reach the office we talk to Rhea about it.

I had my first meeting at a client's place which was now half done; I had some time as we had 15 min refresh and I started asking 'google deity' to suggest me some romantic date ideas for a short trip. After a while, my colleague was looking astonished as it was the first time I was being off focus. He elbowed me, as the break was over and its' time to complete the remaining presentation. We reached the office during lunchtime and told my co-worker to update the reports. Rhea was waiting while I reach her cabin where she just said, "shoot, now!'

"I told her everything as to how are in we have taken things on a slow pace but we also want to splurge quality time with each other. "So, are you in love?" she cried out.

"What No!" "Let's not get there yet! We talk a little stuff about the same. We are not claiming any labels to our relationship. After some time, when we have steadiness, we will name it!" I shrieked, "But you still owe me a treat!" she smiled.

"Rhea, what about Alex, what explanation did you give as to chaos happened?" I inquired. Rhea said that I wanted to make some things clear to him but he suggested that you and he will sort that out. Now, you have to go and clear things out as soon as possible. "Hmm" was the least I could reply. I don't want him to have hopes and not hurt him as well while telling him the facts.

Rhea got a call for an HR discussion from one of our seniors. So, on the way out of her cabin, I just informed you that I will treat you tomorrow or whenever you want as today, I'm having dinner with Mrs.Roy and while going home will do some shopping, I don't have groceries left.

In the evening, I left the office before Rhea and took the subway. I thought of relaxing and having a gala time, so I decide to do some shopping while I order some takeout from my favorite eating spot.

Reached home, and kept the keys on the table. I called Mrs. Roy. She picked up the call, "Hi, you back home!" "Yes!" "I replied. "I will take another 15-20 min to get recharge. Is 8ish fine? Can you come upstairs?" I queried 'OH! Sure! See you at dinner!" with that she kept the phone. I had been lucky to have such good people around. While settling all groceries in relevant cabinets and my refrigerator, texted a few messages to clients and after completing the work got changed into a night suit.

The doorbell rang, and I received the door. Mrs.Roy got in a small box of oats and chocolate cookies. "Do try these. I have made them." I did set the dinner table. It was laid-back talks. "So, what's new?" she smiled.

"Nothing much but yes I have a new friend."

"Only friend??" she responded.

We had a small feast of our own, having some pickled vegetables, chicken wings, and a truffle burger. And the dessert was delicious handmade chocolate cookies. "Thank you for a lovely dinner," said Mrs.Roy.

We watched an episode of 'Modern family' and bid goodbye to each other. I clean the kitchen and was lying on the bed. There was a beep on the phone; I knew it was by whom.

"Hi, I was busy the whole day. What about you? Had your dinner?"

"I too had a good day at work. Yes! I had dinner. What about you?" I replied.

"Having now, sometimes these photo shoots can get boring if we don't get the right click. I will be back tomorrow evening. Let's have dinner together." Kevin replied back

"Sure. I will come to pick you up if don't mind." I asked

"Okay!" "Oh! Yeah! Before I forget; can I book a lakeside cabin at Lake Sebago?"

"Okay! I will plan other stuff" "Please text me tomorrow's flight details as well." I replied again. And the texting was on till I got into the snoring world.

The next day was slow, as I worked on some new client profiles' I texted Rhea. "Should I get him flowers while picking him up from the airport?" "What No! old school!"

"Just take him out for dinner to a very romantic place." I got recommended by Rhea.

I completed my work, and wanted to leave early so that at least see if I get him anything; I'm picking him up for the first time and I just wanted to make a surprise. The most common thing we both had was food. I was starving too. Dinner would take time. I got my colleague's car so had to be very careful; wanted him to have belongings as it is…

I took 2 big slices of Margarita pizza as a takeaway as I couldn't think of any else as I wanted to be on time at the airport. While I reached and was waiting, I received a text from Alex, it said "Hi! Hope you're fine." I had some guilt in me; as I had not gotten in touch with Alex since the Ngo's marathon chaos.

There was a knock on the glass window, which brought me back from my thoughts. Kevin was standing near the car with a riotous smile. I just got out of the car and leap towards him for a hug. We didn't say anything for while…

I realized that we were at the airport and let go of the hug while Kevin gave me a saddened look. I stroke my fingers on my cheeks asking, "So, how was the photo shoot?" and opening the door of the car. With a small smile, Kevin got in, I came to another side on the driving seat and kept his travel bag on the behind seat. While answering, "It was good but guess I got another assignment while I shooting this one!" Kevin did put on the seat belt.

I started the engine; we drove off from the airport. "Why there is a cheesy aroma in the car," Kevin asked. And to which I replied, "Oh! Yes! I forgot. I brought pizza slices as we some time to have dinner." He gave me a cheek peck and said, "Thank you! I was starving!" with that took a sliced box ahead. He took a bite,

"Mmm, this is a good bite." Kevin gave me a foodgasm smile.

"Hey! What about me." Kevin fed me a few bites while driving.

"Can we spend some time in central park? It's nearby" I inquired

"Yes! Let's spend some time there before dinner. We can go home a little or I stay with you. Is that OK? Kevin replied.

I nodded with smile. We reached the park. I stopped the car…

Central Park is habitually visited by tourists and locals alike, this urbanized park is home to countless natural lovely spots and fun-filled activities. We took in the grandeur at Bethesda

Fountain & Terrace wandering through this area before sitting on a bench for some live music and great people-watching. Kevin and I were holding each other's hands. 'I never felt such peace; you know I smile a lot these days. I love my work already but now I feel that I can do more just to make everything stable like I want to fulfill every wish of yours and want you to be happy only with me." "What are you looking at?" Kevin asked me while I was thrilled to look at him. He was saying this all wholeheartedly. "Kevin before any commitment I want us to understand each other. I'm keen to know what the future has store in for us but I wanted to be by your side always" I replied with a smile on my face. I could feel the glow on Kevin's face. He moved forward for a kiss. I panicked and gotup, "Let's take a stroll to Conservatory Garden as well…"

"Wait, Rohan" while saying that Kevin got from the seat.

"I like you. I'm ready! Tell me what about you?" Kevin asked holding my hand in his again

"Let's walk…" There was silence. Kevin and I had taken a few steps ahead.

I broke the silence, "I have never been in a relationship before. Don't know the reason! Just was busy with work life. I also don't want to know if you had a past relationship and why did they fail. With every situation you face and every failed relationship you learn something and use it to improve yourself. You know we are still not normal couples who go through all types of difficult situations so; let's deal with them when they are right in front of us. I like your company too... But, I'm still in nutshell. It's only people around here who know that I have started dating a guy." And there was stillness again for some time. "Oh!" Kevin exclaimed. "Fine, I won't force you to do anything but if you want hide our current feeling. That's not possible. I don't want to be secret..." "Yes! Kevin, I too don't want it that way; so, give me time to sort everything out while we have a few dates before we get for a steady relationship. Is that Okay?" Saying that I put my hand forward, Kevin looked at me for a second and did hold my hand.

"Let's take walk now at the Garden, it has a surplus of trees that truly come alive with vibrant hues during the fall season after that we leave for the restaurant which would be close to your home and will take another 30-40 minutes. I will be hungry soon"

I laughed and we completed the walk and came to where our car was parked. After that, we feasted on 'Steakhouse'.

Reached home; Kevin was already on the couch, eyes about to shut. He kept his bag near the side table.

I was so satisfied when he chose the sofa but now, I want him beside me, "You don't have to do it. There is enough space on the bed. Get up and let's go sleep." I did get changed into my shorts; Kevin came behind me to the bedroom and climbed the bed. As soon as he was in bed, he slept like a baby. "I thank you for today's date. It was lovely. Good night" I said while watching him sleep.

I was so glad that we could talk so much on the very first date. Understanding where we stand in our relationship is so important that I have appreciated it. I too went to sleep; the very next morning, I woke up realizing that we both were spooning each other.

I got into doing daily chorus and came to the kitchen where Kevin was making coffee. "When did you get up? You could have slept a little longer." I know you are late or you will have to wait for me till I get things done and I was up already! so when you were in the bathroom I got up from bed and made coffee for us."

"Thank you," I said while taking the cup of coffee in my hand. "You want to stay or do have work? Can I drop you?" There was a quick reply by Kevin, "You want me to stay?" to which I responded, "Don't get any ideas?" "I just thought you need rest"

"No, I have some work. "Please drop me at 'Brookfield Place'; I have to meet my agent there. There are some projects he wants to discuss."

"OK, then let's leave…" I replied.

After dropping Kevin off, I reached my workplace and started working. The smile on my face was not leaving. I completed almost all the work in the first half itself. My both co-workers gave me weird looks in between.

Rhea dropped in the cabin while I was typing something. "Someone looks in high spirits today. What's the buzz?" "Spill it out!"

"Nothing special; I just picked up Kevin from the airport" I replied without looking up from the laptop.

"And then did something dirty happen?" Rhea grilled

"Rhea"

"Seriously, that's the only thing on your mind" I screech

"No, we had a beautiful evening together and spoke about a lot of stuff. I was happy to get him back; although, it's a work in progress." I said looking up from the laptop. Rhea smiled at me.

"Rhea, What about Alex?" "I didn't call after that!"

He had texted me but I forgot his reply as I was with Kevin picking him up from the airport.

"Call him" saying that Rhea got up from the chair,

"Also do you want me to drop you off today" Rhea questioned.

"No! Kevin is picking me up!" I said.

"Enjoy" Rhea left the cabin

As soon as she left, I dialed Alex's number. It was ringing. He picked after two rings.

"Hi Alex; How are you?" I said from the other end.

"I'm fine. What about you?" he replied

"I'm okay. I'm sorry, hope you understand. I had met Kevin before you and then…" I went on with my side of explaining.

"It's fine. No worries. We can be friends. I knew we didn't click from the very start. Let's just keep in touch…" Kevin replied. I thanked him again for understanding.

"My best wishes are always with you. Now you owe a treat to me and Rhea!"

"Certainly" saying that I hang up the phone

It was a great relief after I had word with Alex. The guilt was off my shoulders. He has been a wonderful person. Thanks to Rhea there is one more friend on the list…

"I will be 10-15 min late" "Will that okay?" I received a text from Kevin

"Yes, it's okay!" I replied back.

In the evening, I could not wait to meet Kevin,

I was at the gate. I knew had to wait for him, so I decided to wait at a nearby café. But to my astonishment, Kevin was at the gate in his 'Versa'.

It is a magical trance that makes everything in life better, brighter, and more beautiful. The feeling is always exciting, overwhelming, and equally surreal for all. However, this is my experience for first-time lovers...

"You said you will be late," I asked while opening the car door and getting in the front seat.

"Work got over soon. I knew its 40 min a drive, so wanted to reach early! Are you not happy?" He glared at me with a wild grin

"Shut up! I was taken aback" "Now drive!" I replied

Now, this had become a circuit, where either Kevin pick's me up from work. We go for a picnic or I drop him at his workplace. I didn't understand how this trial thing worked out for so long...

Sometimes, Kevin had a longer schedule which was throbbing but in end, he uses to make up for it by staying at my place making my whole day jovial. But sometimes we didn't get time; it is only chatting and video calls. Overall, this work in progress was making a real bond between us.

Now, he had a big project coming up, which would take him away for a month and half. We both were restless as this first time he was leaving for so long for work.

"So, don't forget to call me after you reach the hotel" "Please come back soon" I was saying all this while bidding goodbye to Kevin, but he was in some thoughts. "What's wrong?" I said while patting Kevin's shoulder. He smiled and said, "Nothing" "I'm just drained as I'm moving back and forth for work but I guess its fine as long it gets me money."

"I told you to take a break; you wanted to have your small restaurant. You are working to achieve this goal of yours. What about that? I told you that I can take care of finance but you are stubborn." I rebuked

"Rohan"; "Not now! We are going stay apart for while, please let's talk about something else"; after saying that Kevin and I sat in silence inside the car.

Both at the same time, "Sorry" and "I don't like when we have a dispute." "But sometimes I feel we still are strangers; I think you can tell me good things then I should be part of the problems as well. I'm sure; I will not be to solve the problems but if you converse it, you will bite your nails less" I said with a thick smile. You're doing the same thing now.

Kevin smiled and gave me a cheek peck; "How do you?" "Because I…..love…you" saying that I moved towards him to smooch his cheek as well. "Ok. Travel safe. Please call me in between. Let's talk about other stuff when you are back from this shoot."

Kevin once again kissed me on the cheek and opened the door of the car took his luggage, and enter the gate of the airport. He turned one more time and waved his hand; I did the same and started my car to leave the airport.

I had no meetings, so I informed Rhea that I will work from home; while my wheels on the road; I was in thoughts that

'Now, it's high time Kevin needs something of his own. I can see that he is less happy. He just wants to work to be financially independent of me; so, He doesn't have to become a burden on me, but he is not. That's a simple thing! He doesn't get it. There would be adjustments for a few months and everything will be back on track.'

I reached home while working on some of the presentations I search for options for some places to start the restaurant. 'Let me check, if we like it, will go ahead with the plan; for finances will take some aid from known resources.' I thought to myself while researching the places to rent nearby. I will surprise him when he comes back. I was searching for a place nearby the lakeside or park, but that was high on budget. Then, I found a place nearby the city but very quiet lanes'; did send an inquiry for the same. 'Great! Now, wait for the reply.' With that, I returned to my work.

By the time I completed the work, it was evening. I kept the laptop and made some coffee for myself. Sitting on the balcony, I was enjoying the view, the sun was already setting; the building and streets are basked in the pinkish orange sun's light…

I get a call from Rhea, "Hi! So, work done? Did Kevin leave?"

"Hey! Yes, Kevin left! Yes, some days the work is less so we have some time to take it easy. I have something to talk about and I need advice on the same. So, let's have dinner together. Are you okay" I replied.

"Anytime buds!" came back from Rhea.

"See ya!" with that Rhea kept the call.

I'm sure Kevin will love this bolt from the blue. He will happy to see his dream is on its way to being true.

I watch on the couch now, surfing TV, 'How far we have come, Kevin and I? Do we trust each other? We don't each other at all. Halfof the time whether we are with each other and the other it's chatting. We take time to stay connected.' I smiled to myself Now, our lives are one; I feel that we can take the next step by living together. We need to know if we can adjust to each other's company 24/7. I know we can make it. Love can make us do it. People should take this step before so they understand each other more and you know how compatible are with their partner.' 'Look at me the Love guru!' I chatter to myself

The doorbell rang, it was my food order. I didn't feel like cooking today. I wanted simple food; it was an egg cheese bagel with veggie ramen. I had some leftover chocolate cookies from last week's groceries picks. After that, I put some songs and read a book on my bed.

The next morning, I got up my alarm which I put off; sat on my bed for while, and checked if I received any text from Kevin. Yes, I did! It was last night itself.

"Hi, I have reached safely. I was busy unpacking and then took some rest. We will start the shoot soon. We will have rest for tomorrow. Its clothing and men's accessories brand that we have a photo-shoot for. Let me do a video call!"

Checked I missed his call as well. Why I slept early?

"Aghhh." I sighed, missing him already. There is a month to go...!" "Buck up" I sympathized.

"Good morning! Sorry missed your call. I will have a meeting back-to-back; will call you at lunch." I text back and got up to finish my usual norm.

Reaching the office, the first thing I received was a text which made me get a wild smile on my face.

It was from the owner of the place which I had seen yesterday online for the restaurant. "Hi, Hailey this side; I see you have shown interest in the place. Wanted to check, when can you visit the place?"

I replied, "Can I visit this Saturday?" to which there was a reply, "Yes. Please visit by 11.30 am. I'm texting you the proper address to the location".

"Sure" I replied and kept my phone on the table, opening my laptop. I started interpreting financial documents and projections for major clients. Also was updating regular clients' portfolios. I wanted complete this work before Thursday, so Friday I don't have any major work; so, I can also visit monetary firms to understand financial lending."

My work was about to finish, I text Rhea about the dinner plans and she confirmed it.

We were at 'Palace Gourmet' to have a hot pot and some seafood. "So, what's the highlight of your weekday, so far?" I inquire to which Rhea responds, "Nothing much. There is major hiring going on for other branches as well, and have a lot of work. What's with you?"

"I'm thinking of buying a place for a restaurant and gift it to Kevin. I will take some financial help. I'm visiting a place for a restaurant" Rhea almost choked on her food, "Are you nuts? Did you have word with Kevin before taking this vast action; And what if he says No? Is he ready to take up this decision; you cannot just put your opinions on him." "Rhea, hold your horses! I called you about the same. I am taking it to step by step. I have a month to settle the deal, I know Kevin; he will never take it up. It's because we are also at the crest of a relationship. He feels that he already gives less time to me. Sometimes, he is a freeloader at my house but that is not a fact. If I forget, he pays utility bills. Sometimes, we both do grocery shopping. We are almost this married couple who are just staying in different houses because we feel that we can kill each other's personal space. But this time, I feel it's different, now we both want to see each other when we first get up in the morning and cuddle each other almost every night. Somewhere, I can sense that Kevin is aware of the same."

"Wait a minute!" Rhea interfered. Her eyes widened, "Are you going to propose Kevin?"

I just smiled at the thought; "Maybe!" that was my only reply. We left the place and Rhea treats me to ice cream from 'Chinatown Ice cream Factory'. We reached home.

The next few days were quite busy, work kept me busy and the other part was making arrangements. Finally, it was Saturday. I met Hailey at the place "This was my dad's place; I can't maintain it so much" saying this she showed me the way to 'The Loft.' It is an adaptable space where urban meets modern, it's attractive; the brink privately on the top floor of the Flatiron Building like open space is preserved with brick walls with skyline views. Sunlight will fill the area duringthe day is welcoming, and the gleam of the city's lights at night are the perfect urban backdrop for dinner and dancing. Hailey and I had a few discuss how I make small areas for making the kitchen section and waiting area. Then we discuss payment. The place is very much a prime location but expensive. I requested her to let me have a negotiation and payment will partially while as a token. Once the registration is done, I will do 3-part payments. "No, that's way too long" was her reply, Hailey. "Please, it's requested. It's our dream that has to be fulfilled. I will pay in 2 parts; the first part after registration; the last installment after 4 months; please!" I said to Hailey.

"Give me a day to think. I will text you soon" Hailey replied. The meeting ended and I wanted to have lunch. I went nearby Macdonald's to grab a meal.

I was so stressed as I didn't catch any reply after the meeting with Hailey. In between, I missed 2-3 video calls from Kevin. But it was for him, I tried him as well but sometimes he was busy.

Work kept me on hold; I was checking some reports sent by my colleague and was looking through my laptop in my office. I stopped for while, and looked out the window, "I guess the offer was not too good. It has been two days; I have still not received any call from Hailey." Instead, I got a text from Kevin, 'Are you ignoring me, it has been almost we couldn't connect. Are you ok?'

I was sad and wanted him to just hug me. I just responded, 'Yeah, I'm fine. What about you? I will call in the evening' There was no reply

I wanted this surprise to work. 'Please, God!' I heave a sigh. If this works, Kevin will be a most happy person, and seeing him; I will happier.

There was one more ping, I picked up and had a twinkle in my eyes as soon I read the text, it was

from Hailey, it just said, 'I was out of town for some work, couldn't revert. And yes, we are on with the deal'

I was about to scream but control my emotions and reminded myself that I'm in the office. Finally, I was so excited to announce this to Kevin that I almost wanted him to call and inform but I pin down my feelings as I wanted to see his expression when I tell him about this…

Further few days were so tied up that I completing the office work and other jobs related to the restaurant. I felt that somehow, I was less attached to Kevin. This was the first time; we had not seen each other for so long.

Right now, Kevin hasn't picked up my call as I missed the call twice so he is upset. I overlooked the thought right now as I had to restore some parts of the restaurant. I had made arrangements for some workforce…

I reached the restaurant where the workers had reached. I explained the work. I explained to them about the painting preference; I know what Kevin would want the walls to be like; we all function like robots to renovate a place where all my and Kevin's dreams come true.

My phone rang, and to my excitement it was Kevin. I picked up the call; Kevin stormed, "Where are you? I'm trying to reach you, Rohan; it has been 10 days since we haven't spoken. And our text messages only have concerns of our well-being; there is no cheesy talk." "Forget that! There is no talk at all…"

There was silence on both sides. "You, ok?" I replied only that because this outburst by Kevin was for the first time, there was a long pause on both sides. After a few seconds, Kevin said, "I'm sorry! I should have controlled my tone. I miss you…"

While he was talking, 'we are done for today' a voice came from my back. I hold the call for a minute; thank the workers, and caution them to be on time tomorrow as well for the final touches. I got back on call, "Kevin, you there?"

But there was no reply as Kevin end the phone call. I sigh; 'Sometimes, staying apart is very difficult. "Change comes with both fear and some pain. And these two ingredients can create mistrust, misunderstanding, and misinformation. A lot of disagreements are born from them. The only key to solving this communication which lacking...

I have to be patient because if we both lose it; there will be no solution. I was transported into veracity by call. It had been some time, I had not called mom as well; I pick the call, "Hi Ma, how are you and dad? How is everything?" I guess with my tone mom could get that I was saddened. She asked, "Are you ok? Everything is good at work?" I exhale noisily, "Yes mom, the work has kept me up lately. That is why I sound fatigued. Don't worry?" to which mom replied, "Ok. Please take some rest; don't overburden yourself!" We small talk about other stuff and then end the call.

I needed someone to listen so I call Rhea, my only go-to person was her; there were 1-2 rings when she picks the call, 'Hey! What's up? How far is the work done? Did you talk to Kevin?" to which I exasperate; "Rhea!" "Please listen!" and Rhea said, "OK"

"Kevin and I had a small dispute, rather some miscommunication. Nevertheless, can I take off? I just want to take a break from work?"

Rhea with concern, "Are you ok? Do you want me to come over?"

I reply, "No I'm fine... Just wanted some time alone…"

"Ok, it's Friday! I guess you don't have a meeting lined up, only a clerical job is left. You can handle that. We meet on Monday?" Rhea completes the converse.

The next day, I get up lazily, completing my daily task I reach the site. We had final touches to see every task is complete; the restaurant has to be in preparation; so, Kevin can start it almost immediately. We conclude by setting the lounges and table. I pay the workers.

Sitting on the couch, I feel satisfied with the work done; 'Can't wait to see you, Kevin! You will love the surprise and then you will forget everything. And then hug me tight, we will never depart" I close the space with hope; leaving to get home.

While I was at the door, Mrs. Roy came; she had brought home-based pasta, "So, how was the day?" with that query we both enter the house, I hand Mrs.Roy a 'Grapefruit zinger' and take one for myself. We sit on the sofa, "The day was packed with actions. As, I told you will be doing final stuff for the restaurant, and now I'm whacked. I just want Kevin to find the surprise soon. I can't…" on which Mrs. Roy, "told you so; you have found your fondness soon. I'm happy for you. But, remember long-lasting love comes from an open, loving heart." "Love is enduring. It always protects, always trusts, and always perseveres. Love never fails. I believe that two people are connected by the heart, and it doesn't matter what you do, or who you are, or where you live; there are no boundaries orbarriers if two people are destined to be together. Stay strong…"

I felt nice after listening to Mrs.Roy "Thank you! I needed this talk…" I thanked her for the pasta and she left.

I relaxed for while... I was laptop working on a client's investment plan for his new venture; I look up the date, and to my awareness, it had been a month; Kevin will return in another 2-3 days.

After working for some time, I call Rhea to update her that the work is done; if she wants to visit the place. She agrees on the same. Also, put in a request to let Alex join her which I accept. With that, we hang up and surf some series to watch while eating the pasta.

I also send a random text to Kevin, 'Hey, miss you! When are you coming back? Don't forget to send me flight details" to which I get only 'OK' as the answer.

I, Rhea, and Alex meet after a long time. I invited them to the restaurant so that they can observe and remark on the work done. The kitchen was set but I wanted Kevin to have first-hand on the same. Hence made arrangements for some food and beer; Rhea was peeking at every corner of the place. Meanwhile, Alex said, "I'm happy for you. Kevin is the lucky one!" to which smiled. Then we have 3-4 rounds of drinks. Rhea comes back from the trail; we put on some music and sit lounge where Alex sat beside me. We were a little tipsy, the music made body do jiggle. Rhea gets a call; she did excuse herself giving me a wide smile. While we were doing the talk, Alex was close to me, looking into my eyes, he put a hand on my shoulder and came close; I was taken aback. And then there was a roar, "What the hell, Rohan?" Kevin was standing right at the entrance. I was shaking instead of surprised. Rhea came outside when she heard the noise.

"I thought of giving you but thanks for giving me a SURPRISE; how could you? That day when I called, he was the sound that came from behind, right?"

Before I could say anything, Kevin absconded and I stood still.

Rhea quivered to me, "What are waiting for? Just go. He will get the wrong impression of the situation. Please explain things right now!"

I run down, through the streets; Kevin was not seen. I got a little further. He crossed to the other side. I call him, "Kevin" and looked at him from the other side. While waiting on the other side of the road he had been desperate with anxiety and fear, but slowly now there was relief that both were sweeping which was an irrepressible joy that could only be love. Sluggish, we move towards each other. Now, we are close to each other, "Are you trying to put me away?" saying that to Kevin I hold his jacket, to which Kevin held my hands and now there was no need for words, his lip found mine and we kissed. So, we know conclusively that we both were in love.

There was a major honk that scared both of us and broke the kiss. The man from the car, "Assh**" We don't need a show. Can you not make out the fucking public road, now excuse the road. Get aside!" which make us realize we were in the middle of the road.

We move to the side of the road, and looking at each other we burst into laughter. We slowly walk hand in hand, "Kevin, what happened." You reacted so abrasively. But, wait a minute, how did know that we were here?"

Kevin replied, "My work got finished early, I wanted to give you a surprise. I ask Rhea for today's schedule but she gave me the address to this location then I saw you with Alex! I was annoyed!"

I explained, "Mr. Jealous! Did you not see Rhea as well?"

Kevin inquired, "What were you doing there?"

In this chaos, I forgot about the surprise.

"Oh! That's a surprise for you. But let me inform Rhea that we are okay. I also need to take keys from her as I have to tell her to close the place." I said to Kevin while calling Rhea and asking her to meet downstairs.

Alex, Rhea come down, we meet. Kevin said, "Sorry, I act impulsively. Pardon me for my behavior. Rhea smacks his shoulder, "Don't you upset my friend. He has done a big thing for you!" to which I reply, "Shhh, I bring him tomorrow here. Now let's wrap up for the day. Alex thanks for coming. Sorry once again. Rhea, Monday I attend a meeting with Mr. Falcon and then come to the office." With that, we bid goodbye.

Alex and Rhea leave together in Rhea's car. Kevin for while walking asked me, "My house is another 20 minutes from here. Can you stay at my place today?"

"What? But you never…" I exclaim to which Kevin replied, "Yeah, only for today let's just stay there."

We reached the place; Kevin had the keys to the apartment.

My eyes swirled seeing the studio apartment. While removing my shoes, "Are you nuts? Why do stay at my place? This place is a studio apartment. Just look at it…"

Kevin laughed and replied, " I stay here Rohan, of course with one more PG but Rohan this is house and yours is home. It's convivial" I could just smile…

Kevin asked whether I wanted to have something to which decide to just instant noodles. We take our bowls towards small to the loveseat near the big window where we could the night view. I keep my head on Kevin's shoulder after we complete eating. Kevin suddenly, "Sorry, for my conduct today; I lose control when I see you with someone else. I know that I can trust you very much. In a very short period are so close to each other. You handle me well…. But the past lingers around. I had a very bad and abusive break-up. After that, it took a while for me to muddle through, and then it was decided. I would never fall into a serious relationship but the day I saw you, it clicked…"

"Kevin, I don't want to get into the past if it hurts you, I will never break your trust. Have faith in me"

Kevin couldn't resist, "What's the surprise? I cannot wait…"

"OH! Good that you reminded me, we will get up early tomorrow so that I take you there and we spent the entire day laid back…" I replied.

Kevin pulled me closer; almost roughly against, and once again his lips were on mine, kissing fiercely and possessively but now the fear of losing each other was gone.

The next day, we both were excited; we reach the restaurant; I close Kevin's eyes and we walk through the entrance. I remove my hand from his eyes; Kevin looks around with astonishment, "Have you booked the whole place just for the two of us?"

I smile at him, remove the papers and hand them over to him, "Yes, this place is booked for Mr. Kevin as a restaurant owner."

Kevin did not react, I snapped him back into reality, "Hello, Kevin. I'm here. Where are you?" He replied, "Shut up. Don't you dare tease me like that...!"

I reply, "You said you trust me; I put my trust in you as well. I'm sure you will be best"

Kevin came close squeezing me tightly, "How could you do anything so incredibly?" "Ok, now I need to breathe," I reply to which Kevin elude the grip and take a stroll of the place. "I did some small renovations. Hope it is according to your preference."

"Get out of here, Thank you. I will make it big for us!" His facial expression changed, "Wait a minute. How did you pay?"

"No worries, I had some amount saved and the other is a loan." "We both are going to repay it" Kevin replied.

I gave the keys to Kevin who closes the entrance and we spent the entire together….

Now, it has been a couple of months, and Kevin loves his work. He nailed two group events. He shifted all his stuff to our house. He still kept house for an urgent crisis. He experiments with food and makes me taste it to approve it; I work and then go to the restaurant sometimes, to pick up Kevin. I get small surprises when I come home from work to find Kevin waiting. He occasionally helps me with presentations. We have got together with Rhea and Alex. Sometimes, we had dinner with Mrs.Roy.

Everything was on track; it hassles at times but Kevin made it worth it. I had spoken to Kevin's sister 1-2 times; she only family for Kevin. I stillhad not gathered the strength to introduce mom and Kevin. And he was never forced to do so…

"Love is almost never simple; I hate you and then I love. It's like I want to throw you off the cliff the rush to the bottom to catch you"

Baby Steps…

"One step is better than no steps. It's the important little baby steps, which teach us, how to grow. Moving up just one small notch will help us more than we know."

My eyes went wide when I did see mom at the front door, while Kevin was in arms about to smooch me again. I pushed Kevin onto the floor, now I was standing in shock and mom was bewildered. "Mom come in, why are you just standing at the door." Kevin picked up the hint and got up from the floor giving me a death glare.

"Are you okay?" my mom asked while entering the living room towards Kevin. I was right behind her with my alert mode on; "Yeah Ma! He is fine; he is a bit clumsy while patting on his shoulder to not say anything. Kevin put forward his hand to shake it with Ma. "Hi! I'm Kevin, Rohan's… "My friend, my friend" I completed the sentence with panic. Kevin gave me another glare.

"Let me get you glass water. Ma, please take a seat on the sofa," while saying that I hurried to the kitchen; leaving Kevin and mom together. I felt conscious about the situation, while I filled a glass of water Kevin walked in with the question "What was that?" "A friend?"

"Shhh.." "Can we talk about that later?" "Let's just get out first, I don't want her to get any wrong ideas..." I said.

"Sorry! What??" Kevin snapped.

I requested, "Just give me some time, let just meet mom now"

"hmm" Kevin replied and followed me out to the living room

We all were sitting on the sofa after I offered mom water,

"This is a pleasant surprise Ma!" I broke the silence

"Yes! I was missing you; you don't have time for your mother, so I took a flight and came here to stay with you for short time," "You know dad can't stay with me, but he insisted on me a visit..." mom spoke which made me give a startled look. "I was surprised too" mom replied to my expression.

"Did you have something on the plane?" "Shall cook something for you?" I asked "Wow! I would love to…! But now I am too tired. I would freshen up and take some rest." she exclaimed.

While she getting fresh, I asked Kevin, "We will have to stay separate as long as mom is with us" I warned Kevin.

"What?? You're still hiding it from your very own mother; c'mon this is not wise. She loves you and has every right to know! Please don't do this to her…" Kevin pleaded. "I'm sorry but I have to; I only have her and what if she doesn't understand, I might lose her. I don't want her to let down. Once she leaves, we will have our normal lives…"

Kevin said nothing and went to the bedroom. I went to the kitchen, and while I was preparing coffee; mom came in after getting refreshed. "How is it here? Are you happy with your work?"

"I would like to Times Square and Statue of Liberty, as will have less time to explore…" Mom demanded.

"Work is fine Ma," I said while stirring the coffee. "Wait! What? Why do you have less time to travel?" I exclaimed.

"You know your dad! He is mad at you and when I mentioned I wanted to meet you. He warned me that I cannot stay more the week. The major task given is making you say 'Yes' to marriage" mom explained.

"Ma." to which she replied, "Don't 'Ma' me; I have come here to chillax, so we enjoy my stay here and talk about other stuff before I leave. Is that OK?" I nodded my head and hug her tight. "Oh! My sweet baby" she hugged me back. We were in the living room, talking and planning the next few days. "Where is Kevin? Does he have work?" mom asked.

"No, I will just check, he must be on a call" saying I went to the bedroom. He was not there; I looked in the washroom as well. I came back to the bedroom, I missed that his suitcase was out and he was standing on the balcony. "Kevin, why are doing this?" I pleaded.

"Listen, I don't want to start anything with a lie; I'm aware that you have a special bond with your mom; But what about me?" "If I want to make a connection with her; don't you think it's the right time? We can utilize this time to reveal our 'love' to her. She can accept us only if she gets aware of it…" he said and came into the bedroom while I followed. "See I have packed some stuff; I give you three days; let's work this out together!" He went to the living room and sat on the couch with mom. "Kevin, right? How old are you?" "What do you pursue living?" Does my son help you with work?" to that question Kevin gave a bright smile; "Hey! Don't.! Ma, I help him a lot!" I answer that question before Kevin. But that is not true, whenever he stays here. He did major of the chores. Now that he shifted to our house. He completes all household tasks leaving me to pay off only utility bills, and he only reminds me of the same to complete those responsibilities. 'As I said good cook, good looks! What else do I need" Kevin snapped me back from the thoughts. Kevin hinted mom is asking something, "Yes Ma!" I replied. "Can we let Kevin join the trip?" mom insisted. "Mom did Kevin mention he owns a small restaurant that has to be taken care of!" "Whatever!" Kevin retorts making faces. "You're making night feast: once again Kevin while sticking his tongue out. "Mom', "Hope you don't mind me calling you that." "I will take leave now, complete my work and come back before dinner." "I will have to make some provision as well so I can

take off for a picnic". "Sure!" mom replied and waved at Kevin who waved back and left closing the front door.

"So, what's the menu?" Mom said that she took her phone in hand. "I will help too. But let me make a call to your dad" 'OK' I reply and go to the kitchen.

I wanted to keep it simple so prepared lemon coriander soup, mac and cheese with some grilled vegetables. We had some frozen nuggets as well. I started cutting veggies, while mom entered the kitchen. We did our usual talk and I suggest to her that tomorrow she can meet Mrs.Roy and spend time with her. I complete the work and take off on Friday… We can go out on Friday, Saturday and Sunday will rest. Monday again I will take a half day so I can drop you at the airport.

"Are you pushing me away?" mom whispered mischievously.

"Ma, you know! I don't want you to go so soon. But then dad will never agree to this. He has booked the return journey beforehand." To which mom gave me a defiant stare. "I overheard the conversation between you and dad." "But that's not the point. You could stay here for while. I have some important things to tell…"

With that, I get a call from a colleague regarding some work that takes more time. While I complete the call and come to the kitchen; everything is cleaned. The counter is also spotless.

"Ma, I could do it." Taking the hot pan from her hands

"It's ok. You did all the cooking. I can do this much" she replied

I didn't know how the time passed while I chatting with her after so long and the doorbell rang. I open the door, and Kevin was at door. "You are early; you had a big group booking today." He kissed me on the cheeks, "It's done. The other stuff will handle by co-workers" and he came in. I just if mom didn't catch this act." I go after him.

Mom after seeing Kevin said, "Welcome back; that was quick!" "There are some benefits of being owner" she smiled. Kevin winked at me and I glared at him. The next few days went off well; mom and Mrs.Roy became friends after I introduce them. They had failed to notice even if I'm with them; just praying to God that Kevin must have forgotten the two-day warning as well.

It was Friday, I was ready. Mom was waiting for Mrs.Roy as she had invited her as well. I was balcony making Rhea understand, "Rhea, the plan was vague. We plan something next time." "OK, I'm letting off this time. But I will come with you to the airport when your mom is leaving." She ended the call. I didn't realize that Kevin was beside me. He cleared his throat, "Do you remember my request!" "After the trip, I will stay at my place."

"Kevin... Just promise me that if you are coming home with us from the trip, I will at least try and talk to mom." I appealed.

After that talk, we all gather in the living room, Kevin and I picked up the picnic bags. Kevin went ahead followed by Mom and Mrs.Roy... I checked that every appliance and machine is unplugged. The house was neat, and also kitchen top is clean. I gave final look and locked the front door. We all were inside Kevin's cars with Mrs.Roy as tour guide; explaining the history and culture of each street. Kevin had put on some light music. While I was in the front seat, Kevin, of course, made his advances and I was checking if mom is noticing; found her giving 1-2 fixed stares in between. I was a little tense; while I was looking outside the window I receive a call from Hailey, 'Hey! How are you? I speak to her and keep the phone. I tell Kevin that she called for the last payment.

Cruises bring us Liberty Island. We reach the Statue of Liberty; I had been there a couple of times but not as a complete family picnic. It is the number one attraction in NYC. We all were staring at the amazing view of Manhattan. We go inside too, there is a lift which brings you to the first floor it was picturesque.

After that, we come down, and we take a lot of pictures; I tell Kevin to click with me and mom together. I, Mrs.Roy, and mom stand together where Kevin takes a few more after that Kevin takes a family selfie. He comes near to show the clicked pictures. When both gals were engrossed in pictures, Kevin's hands work on my waist and he gives me a cheek peck. "We are on a family date," he says with a wink. I nip his hand, "Yeah! With my mom...How shameless are you?"

Mrs.Roy alerted me that we are taking a walk; you guys can have a few more clicks. Kevin smile and took me to the other. He has taken a lot of candid pictures; I love to watch him do that; he is so happy. We then catch up with mom and Mrs.Roy and bid goodbye to the place.

We have good lunch at Kevin's favorite restaurant. And stroll to street markets and malls. The time was spent well. In the evening we reach, Central Park. I and Kevin never visited the Zoo, so we explore it today; More than a million visitors a year flock here for quality time with some 130 species that inhabit this 6.5-acre corner of Central Park. They have snow leopards, penguins, and sea lions as well. Some children were enjoying observing jungle frogs, poison-dart frogs, Surinam toads, and tons of other little critters.

Budding cherry blossoms are one of the prettiest seasonal signifiers that spring in NYC is in full swing. Here are a handful of spots in the city where you can see cherry blossoms, and one of our favorites is Central Park. We are all this beautiful tour to see these trees.

Our final stop was Times Square, where we enjoy the evening and we love the energy and excitement of the world's most famous block of neon lights.

Now we were heading home, and Kevin stopped the car. Mrs.Roy thanking me for the trip; they come out of the car, I take the bags, and Kevin says, "I'm going to my place." To which I had instantly replied, "I'm telling her right away, please let's go home."

Mrs.Roy went to her flat; we reach ours…

Once everyone was settled, slowly my voice is out, "Ma, I have to say something, Kevin and I are…" I had no words after that to which mom replied, "He is a good choice. But I only approve only when you get married. I will never allow live-in." I was shocked. Kevin smiled. They both had schemed this already. "How did you?" to which mom replied again with wink. **"Kevin is much mature than you, I guess! He explains that** he didn't want to have any wrong impression the whole thing, the first day itself, and we both wanted you to confess..." I hugged her and Kevin after...

It was Monday morning; mom was done with packing; I was already sad that she was leaving soon...

Kevin had to leave early, He hugged mom and wished her a safe journey. Promised her that he will take good care of her son and kissed me on the cheek to which mom scold him, "Little by little; let me get used it...Till then keep away your lovey-dovey stuff away from me..." to which all three burst into laughter.

As decided, Rhea and I drive mom to the airport. "I'm going to miss you Ma. Can you stay a little more?" I hugged her. "I wish... But no worries; I'm happy that you have your own sweet family here; next time I will get more goodies for Mrs..Roy and Rhea" saying that she squeezed Rhea too. Mom left back to our hometown leaving behind so much love...

A few days later, we were enjoying our time watching some movies. The doorbell rang, Kevin opened and Sophia my neighbor was at door. She already had puppyeyes on her face. I knew that I had to be the nanny for a kid for a couple of hours because she had already tricked me twice into this. But I cannot blame her, being a single working parent is a tough task.

I too thought this as I wanted to understand if Kevin would want a family together, back to Sophia; she said, "Oh! Rohan, I am sure you have a guest but I will not be much trouble. I have an emergency shift change, so it will take 4-5 hours. I will come back early as possible. Kevin spontaneously replied, "it's ok. What are neighbors for?" "Don't worry!" to which I looked in shock at him and then gave smile to Sophia while closing the door behind

Kevin carried Elsa on her shoulder while we came inside. As soon as we entered the living room, Elsa started crying. Kevin in panic tone, "I swear; I didn't do anything" I was viciously laughing to which Kevin hit me on my shoulder, "Shut up and do something"

"She must be hungry!" I said to Kevin while taking Elsa from him and patted her back and told Kevin toget some food, "What do you want, noodles?" was his reply.

"No, Kevin! The kid is barely a year and a half. Have look at the table, there will pack meal box of mashed fruits which Sophia gave me." Kevin brought the box and said that he will feed it. I was watching humorously, he trying to feed while Elsa omitted food. Kevin saddened, poor guy. I started slowly with a small story that kept Elsa glued while I hinted to feed her 3-4 spoonfuls. Elsa was playing with her learning toys with Kevin. I was happy to see Kevin doing the activity so well. In while, both were sleepy; Kevin picked up Elsa and sat on the sofa while sat on his lap, holding her grip, they both doze off. I wanted to tell Kevin to go to bed then; I could not control myself taking clicks.

The real fun was when Kevin and Elsa got up. Kevin could smell foul; he had to change her diaper. I roll out on the floor laughing. I helped him later because he was giving death glares.

Meanwhile, we were watching a cartoon, "You're going to be great papa." Kevin said coming closer and kissing"; "And you will be a super daddy" I replied with a wink. Kevin smirked. The doorbell rang, it was Sophia. She apologized for the trouble and thanked me for being such a helpful hand. After we closed the door, Kevin hugged me from behind, "Daddy, huh!" whispered in my ears and he pulled me to the bedroom. We started kissing each other.

Kevin started moving from lips to neck with a sudden halt, "Do you want kids?" I was shocked while looking at Kevin's terrified face. "When the time comes, I know it's way too early. Let's take time for each other." Kevin somewhat had relief on his face and said, "When the time comes…" with that Kevin started kissing my forehead, "Call me daddy!" Kevin teased me again." I slapped him on the shoulders, "You will sleep on the floor", I said sheepishly and Kevin cuddles me more. We sleep in each other's arms…

Time passes by, and now Kevin was so close to me. We don't how stable is our relation; but we are categorizing our romantic status, spending time together, communicating, and working through all challenges together.

I had taken Kevin's car today for work while driving. There was a red signal. I was in the thought that I should take Kevin on a weekend trip. He is always working and we just want to get more time to spend together off our rigid work schedule. A few months back, when we met after a long break. He had surprised me with a sudden plan for Lake Sebago. He had planned everything. The cabin he booked was near the lake. All the cottages are nestled in a half-moon facing the lake. We were going to spend just two days but I was already fallen in love with the place. It had screened porches, comfortably furnished with a fireplace, modern kitchens, and bathrooms.

After settling our stuff in the cabin, we went for a trail walk, diving in the lake, and then watching the sunset together. We came back to the cabin. Kevin had given me bewilderment the cabin was decorated with scented candles. The dinner was arranged by staff. It was Creamy Parmesan Risotto with wine. Kevin pulled me close and kissed me. Slowly, we moved legs together with no music only the sound of the night; Kevin now moved his hands back. I urge him to complete the rest later after dinner.

We just got changed into shorts. I came out of the bathroom and saw Kevin sitting on the sofa. I slowly approached him, sat on his lap started kissing him. He had planned everything; I just had to give in because it was for Kevin.

Kevin kissed asking for permission to kiss with his tongue.

I gave him the space and he was fully charged with started unbuttoning the shirt and then there was a car honk. Back to reality, I drive to the office. But the thought of a weekend trip made me smile and will make it happen soon. I winked and got back to work.

Nowadays, we work hard, so sometimes miss having dinner together or for work, we stay away which makes us crazy.

We are living at a time when we have unprecedented round-the-clock access to one another. Now and then wedevote extensive free time to catching up which can be a tremendous gift; I and Kevin shut down social media and everything to which we are connected to the outer worldand stay home enjoying the time with each other. We like it that way, being in our small world with Kevin cooking and me doing other daily household tasks. After that, we both just listen to music while he reads some books and I lie on his lap practicing some journaling.

But these days; the length of time you will spend texting, talking, or video chatting in a day or week is less. These days Kevin was late from work and sometimes, was tense. I inquired but he ignored the topic. I thought it would have been working pressure.

We were busy with work lives having minimal time for each other. Sometimes, the weekends were intensely packed for Kevin. We have less time these days where we have small arguments and talk about other problem.

As usual, Kevin was late. I was irritated also I was missing spend timing with each other. So, I decided to take the car, drive to Kevin and have dinner together, using up time with each other for a change.

I park the car and make my way toward the building. I see Kevin crossing the street to the building entrance. I follow…

I was shocked when I saw Kevin with some stranger. He had an envelope in hand which he gave to the man and they discussed it for a few minutes. After that unfamiliar person kissed Kevin and there was outraged me, "Kevin!" And I came towards them while the stranger left the place before I could say anything; I turn Kevin, "What's wrong with you? Are you cheating on me?"

"I can explain," Kevin said, clearly, I was not in the state of mind, "Yeah! I have seen it with my own eyes. I don't want to hear anything. I was crazy to make you love. I brought this place for you. I work hard and you are thoroughly enjoying the third-wheeling affair. Why?"

I don't want to stay here with you; let's take a break. We will clear our heads. I walk away from there. I reached home before Kevin; I slept in the bedroom.

In the morning, I could not see Kevin anywhere. His stuff was gone too; 'I don't need him as well. How could he leave? He didn't try… What I had seen was real then?"

It had been a few weeks; we both had spoken to each other not even texted. I was on the balcony with my coffee. 'Did I miss something? I don't understand did Kevin kiss that guy? How long they are together? Last few weeks, he was tensed… Was it guilt that he could not tell me; I should encounter him? This way no one stays happy. I don't know… We always sort things out, how could I not do it this time? I was heartbroken!"

The next few days, were lifeless, I was into the routine but like a machine; no emotions at all. My work was hindered. I get to call from Mr. Robin. After that I reach his cabin, I knock at the door; "Come in." was reply.

"Rohan, Have a sit." I pull the chair and take a seat in front of Mr. Robin. "Is everything ok?" You are a promising person but the last two clients are least satisfied with your work. "Why is that so?" I was sitting in silence. "You will have to explain to me something…" Mr. Robin looked at me; I take a deep breath "Sir, I'm sorry that the last few days were tiring due to personal grounds. But, from now on, I will not give you a chance to find fault."

"That's like Rohan. If you need to talk, we are there. Please take care of yourself. I know every now and then work pressures go to the extreme."

I got a workaholic and kept myself busy; I kept my social life very low. Weekend plans with Rhea were almost diminished.

It's been a long time since Mrs.Roy had dinner together so today she called me home for dinner. I didn't say 'No' to her. We had dinner in silence. Following a few morsels, Mrs.Roy said, "Are you ok? You and Kevin"

I look at her with gloomy eyes; slowly explain what happened.

"Rohan, it's incorrect. You should give him a chance to explain. Arguments are an important part of the relationship. It will strengthen you both and ties, because "In true love, the smallest distance is too great, and the greatest distance can be bridged. Now you have to make move"

We complete dinner, Mrs.Roy brings a candy jar but this time she hands me a toffee for the jar. It was flower shape gummy.

I thank Mrs.Roy for the dinner while she waved and said, "Let the love bloom again" to which I give half a smile.

I didn't want to go home, I remember what Kevin said, "This was home and that was a house" I take a lift down.

There was a bar a few streets across, I walk down and then enter the bar. I order some vodka shots. I take 2 shots and then my eyes were just wandering through the bar. I was shaken when I did the same strange face from that night when Kevin and I had a fight.

I pay at the counter and follow the guy. He takes into one of the deserted streets. I guess he got to know that I followed and he turn to bawl, I put all my strength and punch him harder in the face. He yelled, "What the hell? Who are you?"

I interrogate, "How do you know Kevin?"

He gives me a grin, "So you are the one because of which Kevin refuses to patch up. I had to intimidate with our lewd pictures."

I was burning, "But he kissed…" then there was the reply, "No I was about kiss him, I was so close but he put all strength in his hands and push me away then you came. I had to leave because we had a deal that as long, he pays; I will tight lip"

I was about to punch him, but then I didn't want to waste time; I warn him, "That was your last meeting with Kevin. Don't you ever cross him again; I will kill you if you do so!"

And leave the place in vain.

I had to rectify my error. I tried to connect to Kevin but he did not receive my call. Thanks to Rhea, she called and checked on Kevin. He was devastated. He is pure love but now he feels that 'love' is made from him. My concern was solved and was content that Kevin was fine.

A few days later, I visit a nearby restaurant. I call Jacob to check if Kevin was fine and he has kept the restaurant going…

Jacob confirmed that a few weeks back Kevin had trouble, to which he tells him about his abusive boyfriend. He met him accidentally while grocery shopping; the guy followed him and then he used to appear frequently to be a nuisance for Kevin. I was not supposed to tell you this as Kevin had warned but he is more silent these days. I assure Jacob that everything will change and thank him, also tell him to leave otherwise Kevin might doubt.

Now, I have to face him; I should have trusted you, Kevin.

But I'm sure it's not too late; I will try and get you back.

I drove Kevin's car towards the restaurant.

Hoping, Kevin will forgive me. After that, I will propose to him and we will be together forever. No more distance apart us. My thoughts took hold when I reach the restaurant.

I come down to meet Kevin, while I was at the front door; he was working at the counter placing some bottles on the shelf. He turned and looked at me. I realize that I miss him so much. That naughty and sweet appearance of his made me hypnotize. While looking at him, I just started daydreaming about him walking toward me like he is walking down the aisle. Bit by Bit, I started walking towards him and he too got nearer…

"When two hearts become one, it cannot be undone. A promise has been made and cannot be broken or swayed. For this love will last an eternity and will not fade

And The Final Fall for Him...

"Falling in love is easy. Falling in love with the same person repeatedly is extraordinary."

He slapped me, "How could not believe me? I feel the same way; whatever you felt was real and it was equivalent to me. We had decided the way to solve is to talk about it, argue about it and then find a solution to the problem. But you blamed me. You didn't reply to my calls. I waited for a text or call but they never came to me."

"You know back then I gave you a chance to explain… How could do this to me? Did you ever love me, Rohan?"

"I…." as I was about to speak, Kevin stopped me again saying, "Shhh… Don't say a word. Everything you gave me was benign. I thought everything was ours…" Kevin went to the cabin where he kept the official documents of the restaurant. He came and handed it to me. "This was an unconditional and priceless gift for me as it was given by you, who only wish love for me.

But I guess things are different now!" "I don't want to dishonor this place. Not at all! But this will weigh down on my love. So, keep these papers with you until we have the final solution…"

"Kevin, stop. Just listen…Please, I understand that anger doesn't solve anything nor it builds anything. But staying apart from you made me miss you; the more you were absent in my life, the more I missed you, and the more I loved you Yes! I love you more! Sorry! I'm verbalizing this now…!! Your absence has sharpened my love, and now your presence will strengthen it. They say you've found true love when you catch yourself falling in love with the same person over and over again despite them being miles away from you."

I was still for a moment then I removed a small box from the pocket and opened him to show him the ring.

"I'm not giving you the ring at the present, if you need time to answer this question, take a while; this may sound tasteless now, but when you answer this; I will relish all the flavors in our life" "You deserve the world and all the good things it has to offer. If I fail to find that, I promise to give you mine! Because every long-lost road led me to where you are. You taught me the real meaning of love. I want you to hold my hand tight as I want to grow old with you from this day forth. You bring out the best in me and now please give me a chance to be the luckiest man alive." saying that I handed the papers to Kevin.

"You say that now, I…I need time; we both should take up space. Let's clear our heads; till then I stay at my place. About the restaurant, we talk about it later. Right now, I don't snatch my co-worker's living. They have taken an effort to make this restaurant" Kevin answered.

"Fine, you take time; I will hold. But, one thing; I want to spend our first Christmas together. I will buy tickets for ice skating at 'Rockefeller' and then we watch the Christmas tree. We will have hot chocolate at café 'Grumpy' and then…" I stopped looking at Kevin's glimmering face.

"And then…" Kevin repeated. I smirk, "I will take your leave, for now, it is going to be the hardest but I will wait…" with that I leave the place.

Once he says Yes, I will never leave him. We might have small scuffles again but we solve them by staying together. I cannot stay away from him. That night I slept soundly because now I know what my heart wants.

The next morning, I started with the usual work, but with confidence. I felt charged. My energy was at its peak. I had two meetings which were done well. After that, I was sitting in my room thinking about whether to text Kevin or not. There was a knock at the door; while coming in; my colleague congratulated and updated me that maybe my position will be upgraded. While we discuss a few pointers for the next project, I was into my thoughts, 'That's nice but I would have well if I share it with someone special.'

Rhea barged in and broke my thoughts. My colleague left after the discussion and Rhea sat on the chair across asking, "So, how was it?" I replied with a big smile, "It was astonishing; I felt such relief after talking to Kevin. I'm sure my Christmas will be thrilling. So, let's do window shopping. What say??" Rhea jolted, "Omg! What confidence!" "I trust you, so we will go shopping!" with that she exited the cabin.

I was in my thoughts again, "Christmas is after 20 days. I gave too much time. I hope Kevin does not give up on me. I need one chance…I will stand by forever. We have come so far. Please!

From daydreaming to reality, I took my phone out and texted about the promotion to Kevin. But there was no, reply. I told myself, 'Buck up Mister, It's a long way.'And back to my laptop to complete my work.

Days were passing by; there was the least exchange of words from Kevin. But I was in high hopes, so this weekend we did the shopping. I already thought about the gift; I had told Rhea what I wanted so, took me to the perfect location where I could shop for the same…

Today, I was missing Kevin a lot; I'm sure he will never agree so I decide after work, I visit the restaurant only to see him. I wanted him to make coffee for me; he makes the world's best coffee. It keeps my heart warm. I complete my work and took a cab. 'What should I do? Keep it simple Rohan! No pressure. It's just a cup of coffee.' The honking of the automobile made me come back to reality. As I reached the restaurant, I felt lightened up. My eyes were searching Kevin but in vain. Instead, Jacob one of the serving staff came in as soon as he spotted near the entrance.

Jacob offered a table saying, "Long time Sir, please have seat. What will you have?" I was a little self-conscious to ask about Kevin. "Is Kevin in the kitchen?" to which Jacob replied; "No. He will be coming in while. He had to fill in some groceries. You want anything." I said with a cheerless tone, "Nothing for now. I will wait…" with that Jacob went to do his work.

After a while, Kevin entered, and he overlooked my presence. There were some boxes in his hand. Before I wanted to lend a hand Kevin called his assistant. He then walked to the counter arranging a few things eyeing me in between. Kevin said something to Jacob and he came towards me. "Will you have something?" "I need coffee". I voluble, in return all eyes laid on me.

Jacob took off to the kitchen, and Kevin followed him. I was impatient as no one was coming out from the kitchenette. Thankfully, Jacob came with a cup of coffee. Kevin was still inside. I took a sip of coffee; it was as saline as seawater. I didn't give any reaction. I knew Kevin was watching. I took a second sip. I was above to take the third one. But Kevin came in and held my hand; he took the coffee and gave me another cup. He gave a look, "Drink and then leave." To which I reply, "2 more days, Kevin…" He turned around. I sipped the world's best coffee slowly so that I could watch him for while. I left the place with a sweet smile on my face as I could sense Kevin is melting.

The next two days were like ages. I was preparing for the big day. I was sure he will be there but I was restless. My heart was pounding. I just close my eyes.

The next morning, I didn't even need an alarm. I was up; got to the bathroom and got refreshed, after that I went to the kitchen; had a rye sandwich with some coffee. I made all arrangements and waited for the evening to turn up.

In the evening, I went to Mr. Roy to wish her 'Merry Christmas' "I will get late so wish you right away, and here is a souvenir for you. Thanks for being a part of my life" to which Mrs.Roy replied a box of heart-shaped cookies. She then brought the jar of candies signaling me to grab one! I put my hand in the jar. When took my hand out, it was heart-shaped orange candy. Mrs.Roy smiled and said, "Best wishes" and "Merry Christmas"

I left for the first place Rockefeller's iconic skating rink. It just sparkles. It is pure Christmas magic right before your eyes! I had tickets and was waiting for Kevin. My heart was throbbing. I had texted the details to Kevin, for which there was predictable no reply. My heart sank as I could not see Kevin anywhere; I waited at the rink and was about to kill the ticket but then someone elbowed me, I looked to the left; Kevin was beside me. "You have two tickets?" "Yes," I replied. We both went inside the rink, we started skating, I was not so familiar; went with slow rounds. Kevin started very well and was thoroughly enjoying. I wanted to catch up a little speed but suddenly I fell to balance; tripped on the ground. Kevin came near giggling giving me a hand and said teasingly, "Why are you lying on the ground?" I replied taking his hand while getting up, "I lost something" "What" Kevin asked, "My balance," Kevin ignored, "*You mean you fell?*" to which I replied, "*Yeah! For YOU*" and Kevin blushed. He seems I fail to notice. "OK, enough skating" I'm tired Kevin said.

We came out of the rink and took off our skates. He was admiring the decoration around not giving a glimpse at me. In sudden, I took his hand in mine, we pass through 'Grumpy Cafe' where we had hot chocolate and cleaned Kevin's chocolate mustache to which he said nothing. That's a relief! Kevin did notice a bag in my hand but didn't inquire about anything. "So, what was the last part you didn't mention that day?" to which I smirk "You remember!"

"Let's go" saying I pulled my hand out waited for Kevin to hold it. Slowly his hand came in.

And now we were at Central Park, where old vintage fixture meets the modern. I was walking when I realize Kevin had stopped a few steps behind. I flipside and walk towards Kevin, "Why are we Central Park?" he asked. The glint in his eyes made me recognize that he understood what it meant to us…

I had called a horse carriage for the ride; Kevin was startled by the events happening tonight. We both sat in the carriage, and the drive started. There was long silence…

"Thanks for coming. It signifies a lot." I broke the motionlessness moment. "Hmm; I had to.

What are going to do without me?" I looked at him in shock. Then we both smile. The ride stopped at Fountain I give hand to Kevin and we both reach the bench 'the first confession'

Kevin glances at the bench and then looks at me with shock, "How did you?" I instantly say, "Don't ask. Rhea helps me manage; I see that she has done the job well"

The bench ornamented with flower bouquets around, some purple balloons, and a few colorfultinsel. It was love that surges…

"Come sit" I said to Kevin and we both sat on the bench. I hold Kevin's hands and said, "You know you mean the world to me and no fight is bigger than our love for each other. I feel bad about the way we left things. I know fights and disagreements are part of a relationship. But I want you to know that I'd much rather lose an argument than lose you."

Kevin gaze at me sideways and then gawked at the bag I was carrying for a long…

"What's in that bag?" I laughed it out when Kevin said that; Kevin love surprises. And I love him.

I open the bag take the ring box out, then I take out the gift; it was Crown Cufflinks with Lapel Pin & Tie Pin with customized initials 'R&K" on it. The next souvenir was the couple's wine glass with personalized etch work. I was amazed by the design; it was 'The Laurel leaf wreath with R&K combined between the leaves. And wine bottles too.

Kevin had tears of joy when he had seen the effort made. He said, "Nothing hurts me more than these silly fights driving us apart. Let's strive to create more happy moments from here on." "No matter how much we fight or hurt each other, I will always be there by your side through this journey called life."

I removed both rings and exchange the rings; there were a lot of fireworks in the background. I thought God made it flawless. All things are precise! I look up and thank him, while Kevin takes the wine glass to pour the wine. We take the glass and kiss each other till we were out of breath.

Holding Kevin's hands, I showed him the ring again and said, "This ring is reassurance for how far we have come. I love you Kevin" "I love you too" was the reply.

While we pack the stuff again, I naughty exclaim, "The fight is done, and now I want some hot makeup action. Can't wait to wrap my arms around you and then some ;)"

Kevin smacks me on shoulder, and with that we walk away from the garden through the Christmas lights and carols …

"You call it madness, but I call it love." – … Love starts as a feeling, but to continue is a choice. And I find myself choosing you, more and more every day."

About the Author

Jagruti Gandhi

Jagruti was born and brought up in Mumbai, India. It is a city that never sleeps and always helps us to tackle problems, make friends in just 10 minutes, and also teaches us to behave on a Global Stage. Her passion for writing started at a very young age. Poems were her first friends. The habit of writing got forgotten somewhere after entering the professional world and all the fun and carefree days were left behind. This pandemic taught her new lessons and gave her time to recall the skills of composing. Jagruti is still a work in progress!!And finally, since she has amateur writing skills, she will always appreciate the valuable reading time of her bibliomaniacs!!

www.ingramcontent.com/pod-product-compliance
Lightning Source LLC
LaVergne TN
LVHW041846070526
838199LV00045BA/1455